NINA

IN That Makes Me Mad!

Pur-r-r-r-r

HILARY KNIGHT

STEVEN KROLL

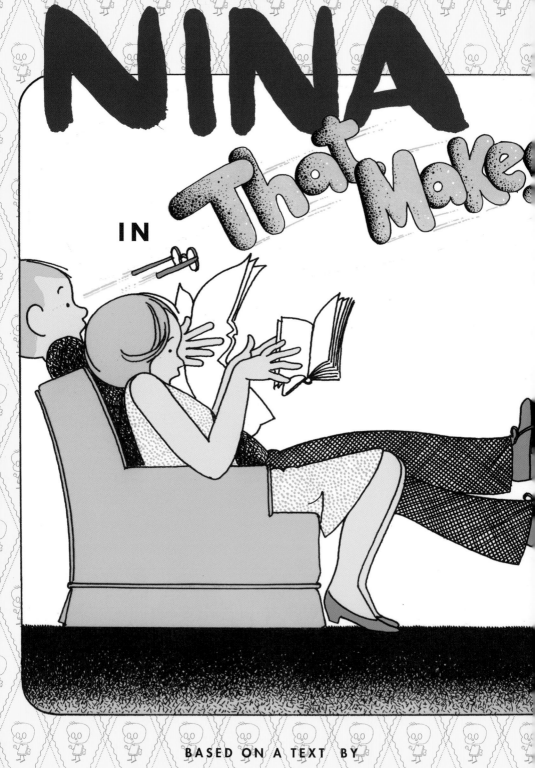

NINA

IN

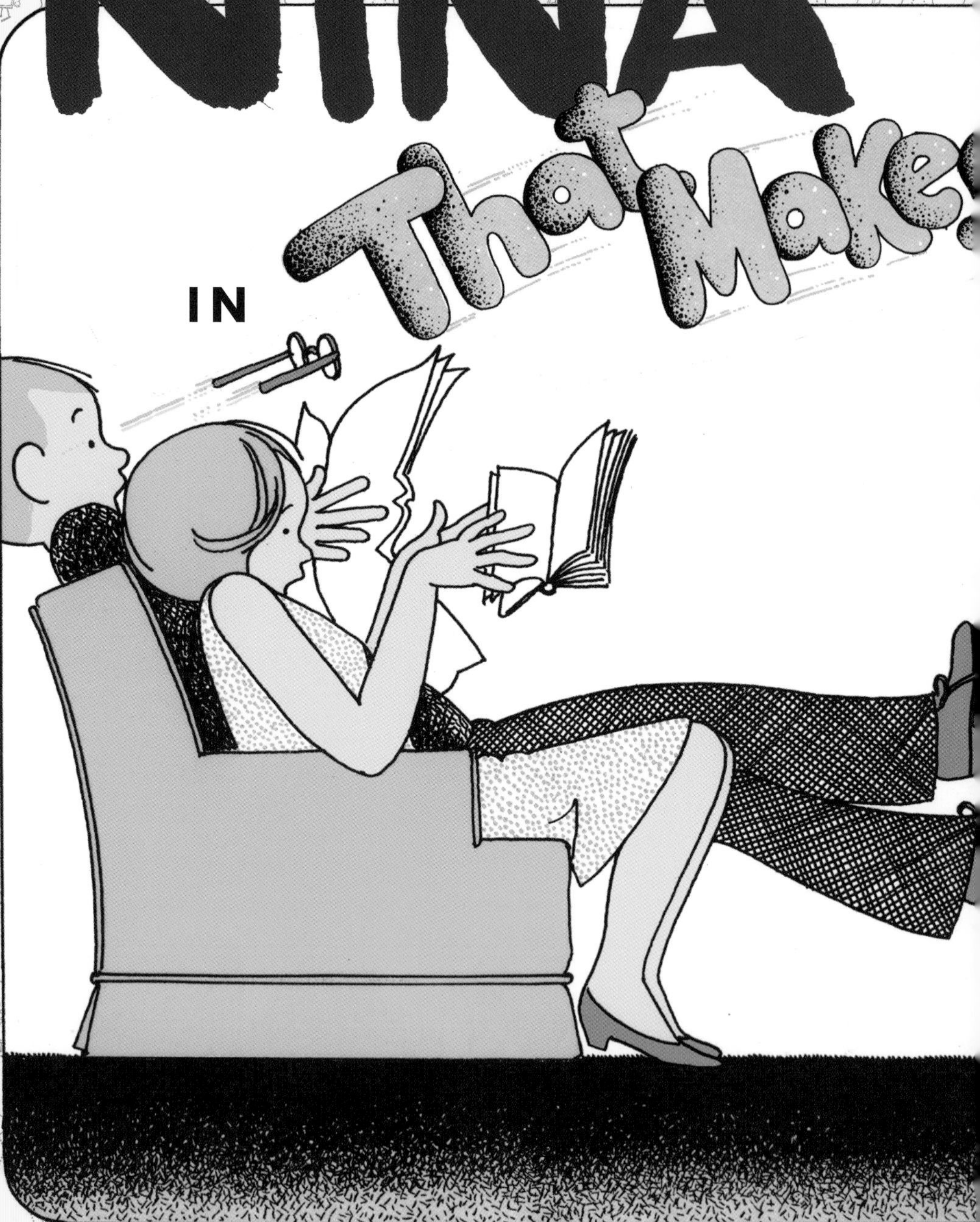

That Makes

BASED ON A TEXT BY

STEVEN KROLL

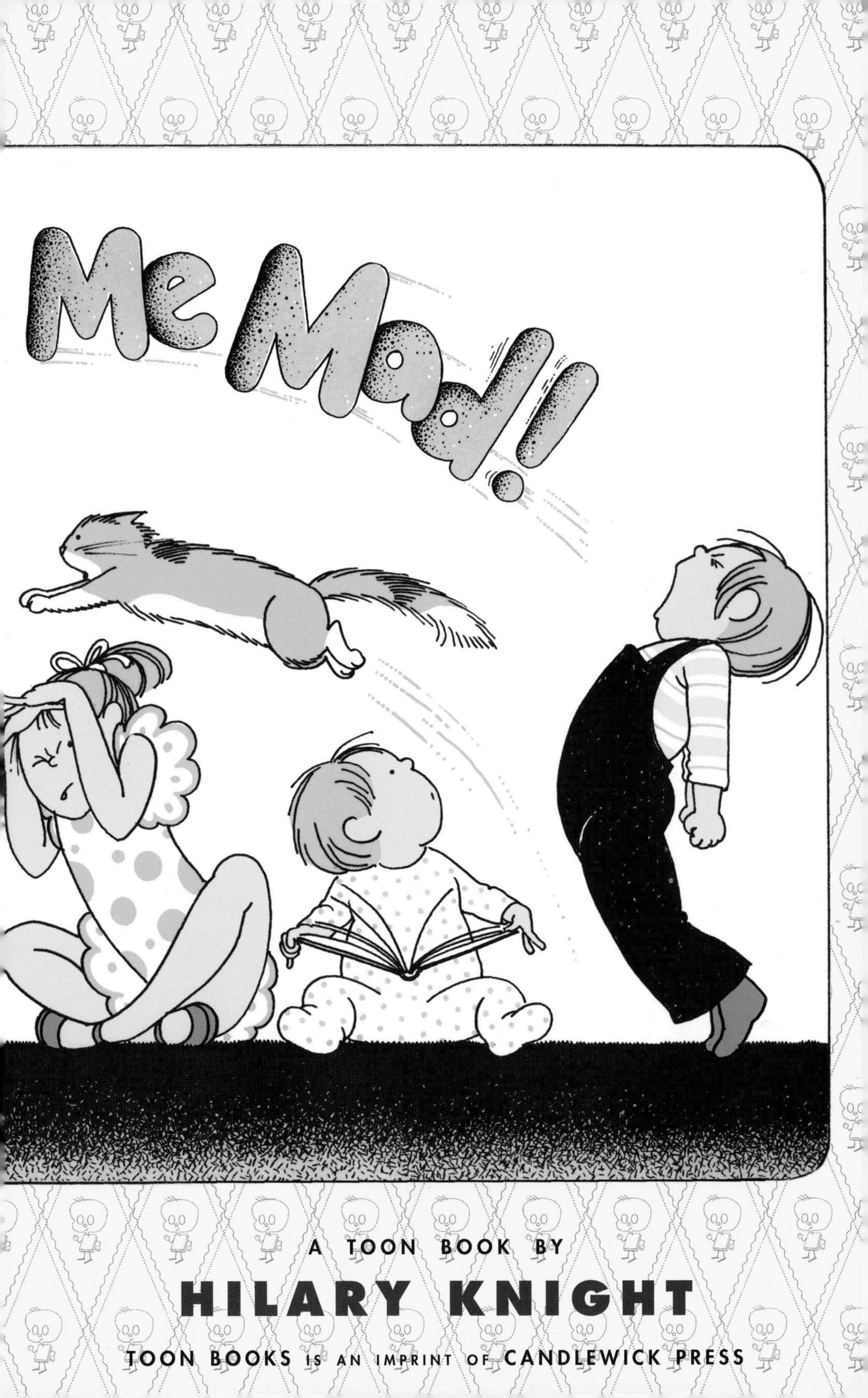
Me Mad!!

A TOON BOOK BY

HILARY KNIGHT

TOON BOOKS IS AN IMPRINT OF CANDLEWICK PRESS

Visit us at www.abdopublishing.com

Reinforced library bound editions published in 2014 by Spotlight, a division of the ABDO Group, PO Box 398166, Minneapolis, MN 55439. Spotlight produces high-quality reinforced library bound editions for schools and libraries. Published by agreement with Raw Junior, LLC. All rights reserved.

Printed in the United States of America, North Mankato, Minnesota.
042013
092013
This book contains at least 10% recycled material.

For my father, Clayton Knight *-Hilary Knight*

For Kathleen. Forever. *-Steven Kroll*

In memory of Steven Kroll (1941-2011),
a beloved and long-time member of the children's book community.

Editorial Director: FRANÇOISE MOULY

Book Design: FRANÇOISE MOULY & LAURA FOXGROVER

A TOON BOOK

Library of Congress Cataloging-in-Publication Data
This book was previously cataloged with the following information:

Knight, Hilary.
Nina in That makes me mad: a TOON book / by Hilary Knight ; based on a text by Steven Kroll.
p. cm. -- (TOON Books)
Summary: Lots of little, everyday frustrations make Nina mad, and she is very good at expressing her feelings.
[1. Graphic novels. 2. Anger-- Fiction. 3. Behavior-- Fiction.]
I. Kroll, Steven. II. Title. III. Title: That makes me mad.
PZ7.7.K66Ni 2011
741.5'973--dc22

2011000802

ISBN 978-1-61479-153-9 (reinforced library bound edition)

Spotlight

All Spotlight books are reinforced library bindings and manufactured in the United States of America.

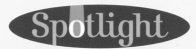

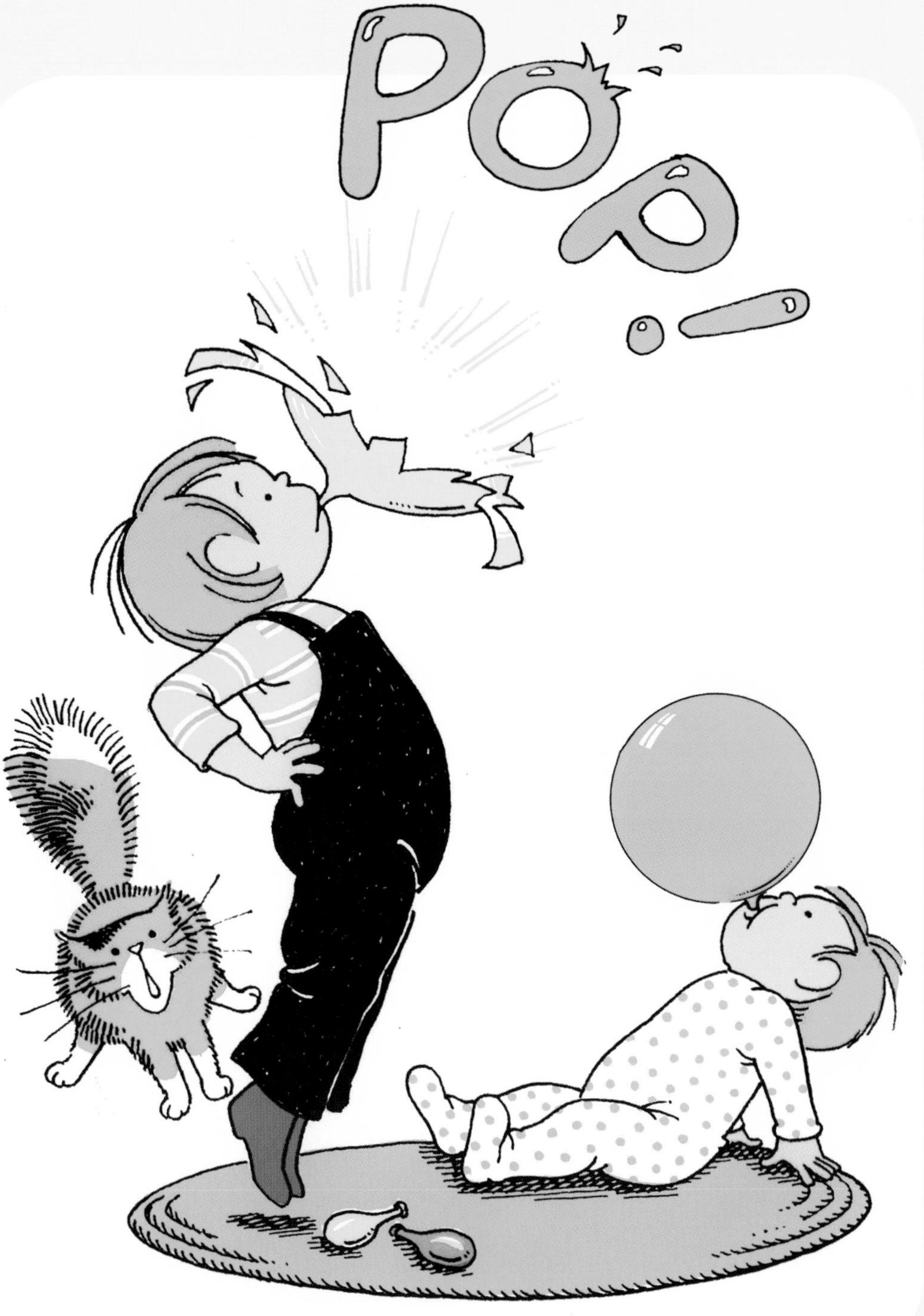
POP!

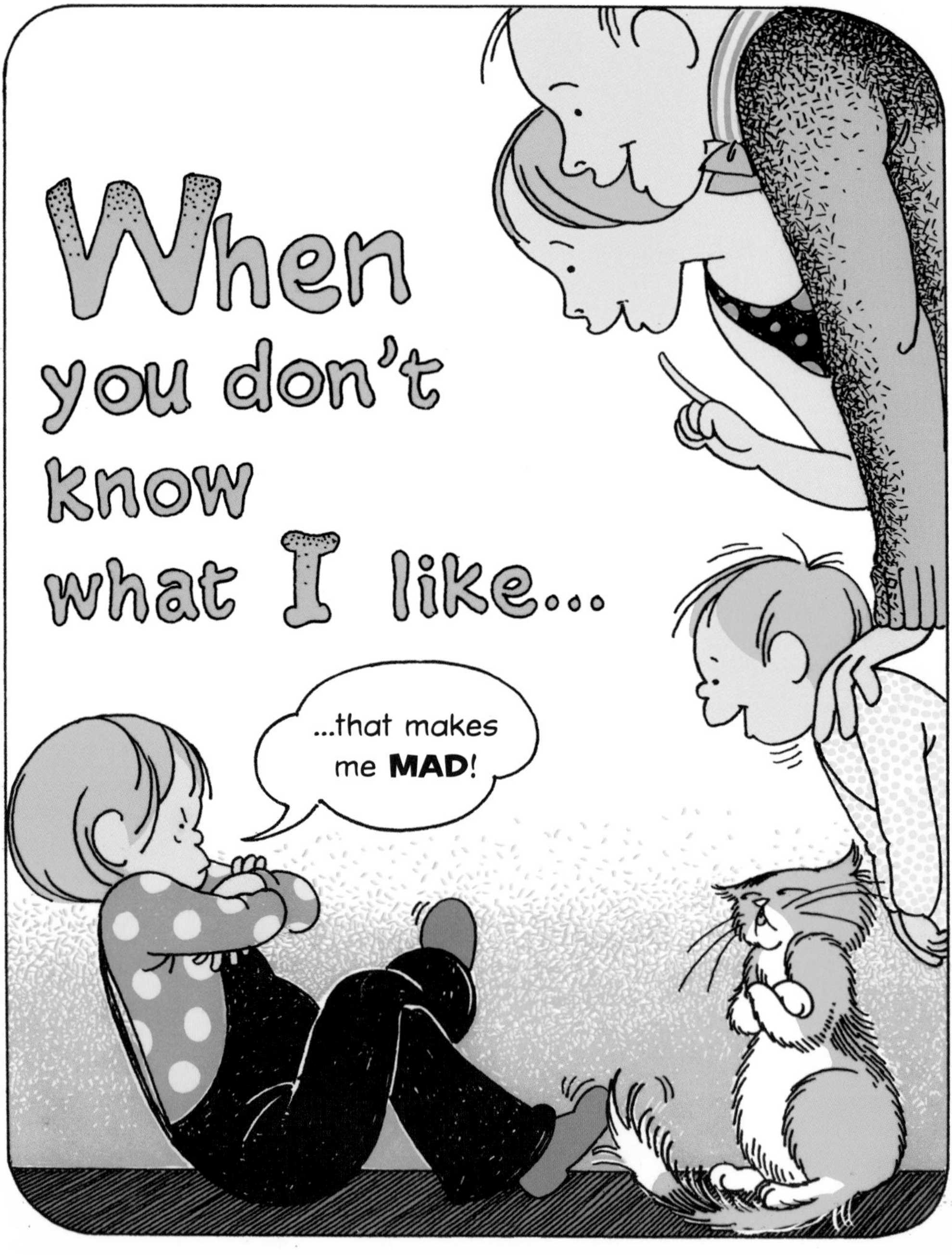
When you don't know what I like...
...that makes me **MAD**!

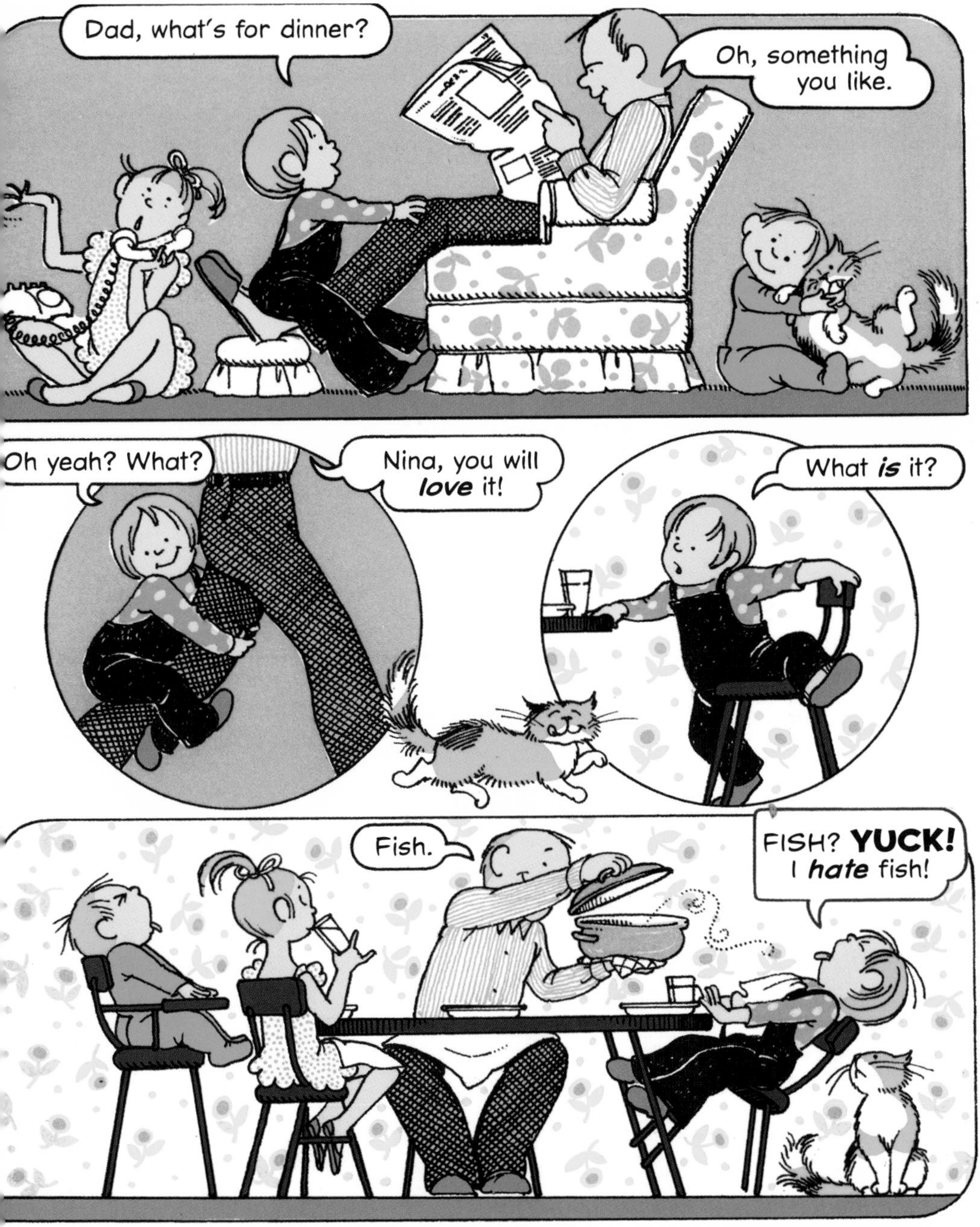
Dad, what's for dinner?
Oh, something you like.
Oh yeah? What?
Nina, you will *love* it!
What *is* it?
Fish.
FISH? **YUCK!** I *hate* fish!

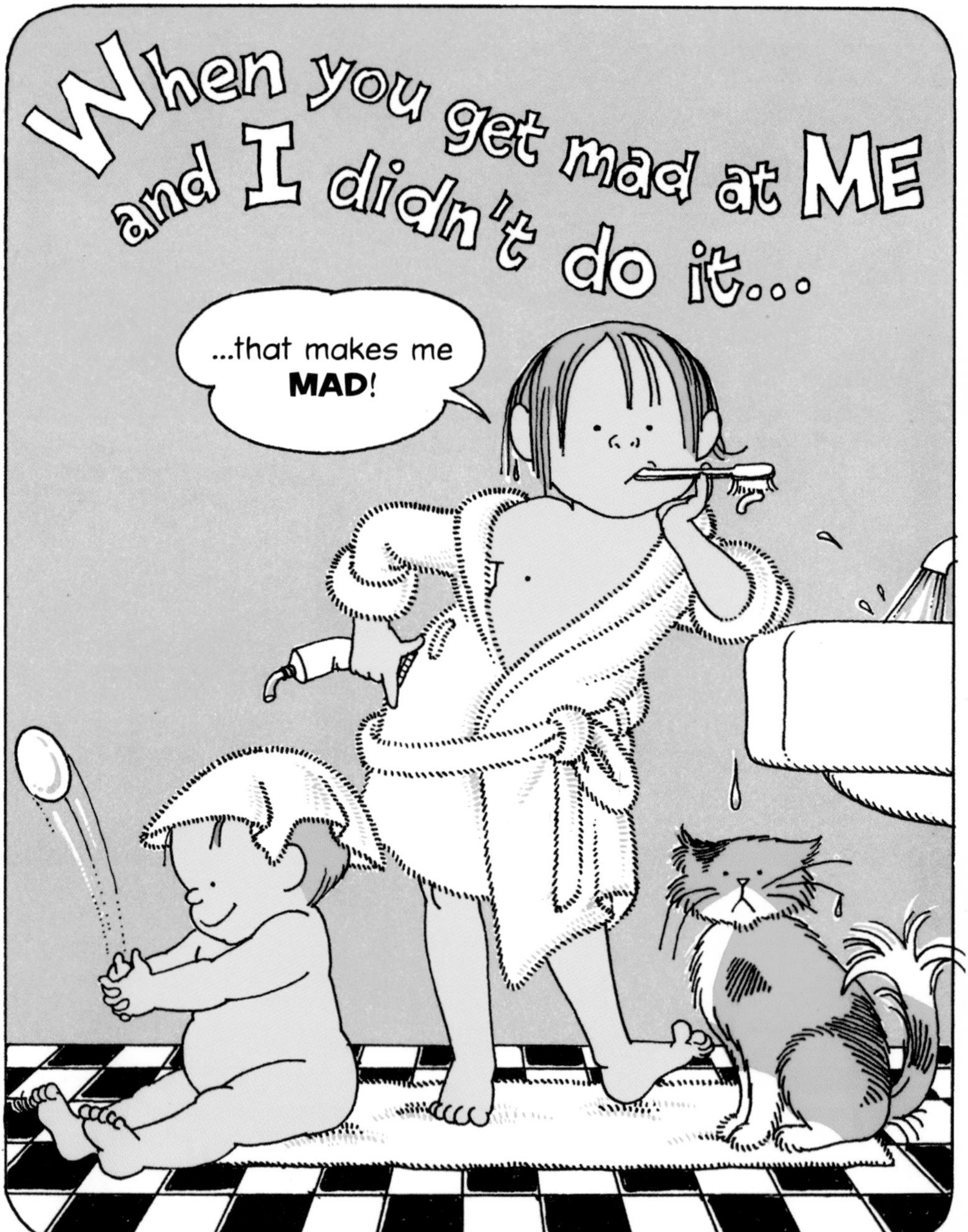
When you get mad at ME and I didn't do it...
...that makes me MAD!

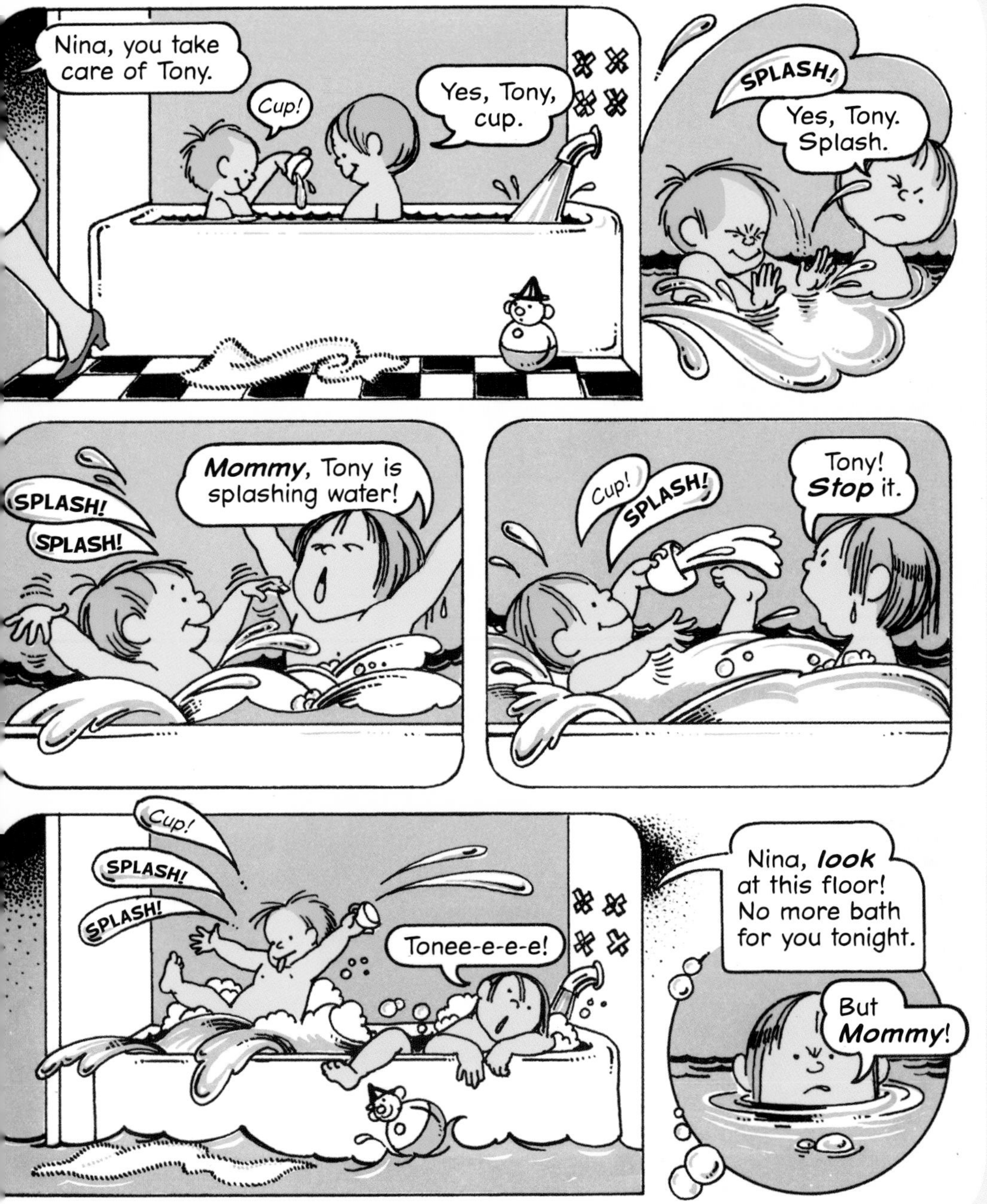
Nina, you take care of Tony.
Cup!
Yes, Tony, cup.
SPLASH!
Yes, Tony. Splash.
SPLASH!
SPLASH!
Mommy, Tony is splashing water!
Cup!
SPLASH!
Tony! Stop it.
Cup!
SPLASH!
SPLASH!
Tonee-e-e-e!
Nina, look at this floor! No more bath for you tonight.
But Mommy!

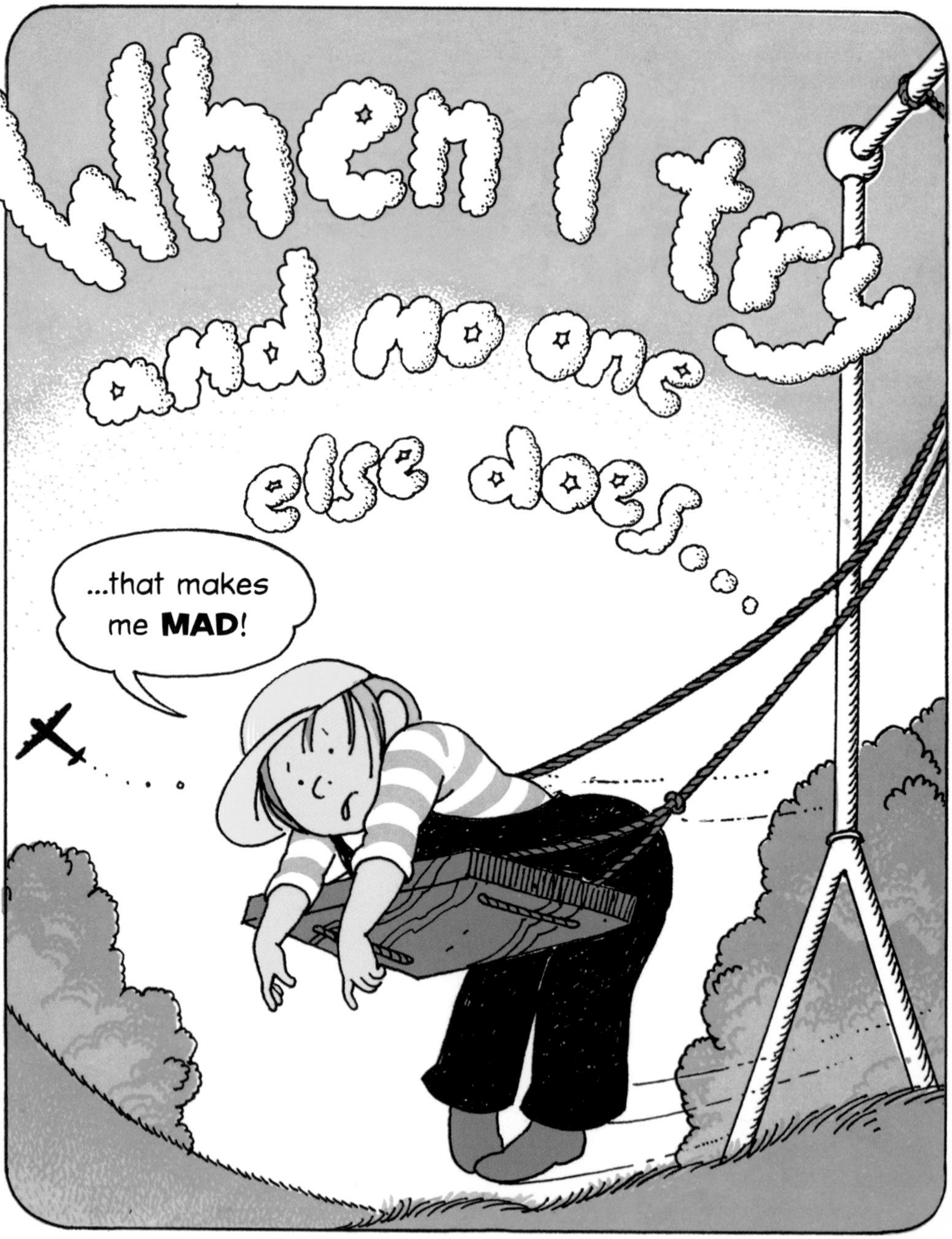
When I try and no one else does...
...that makes me **MAD**!

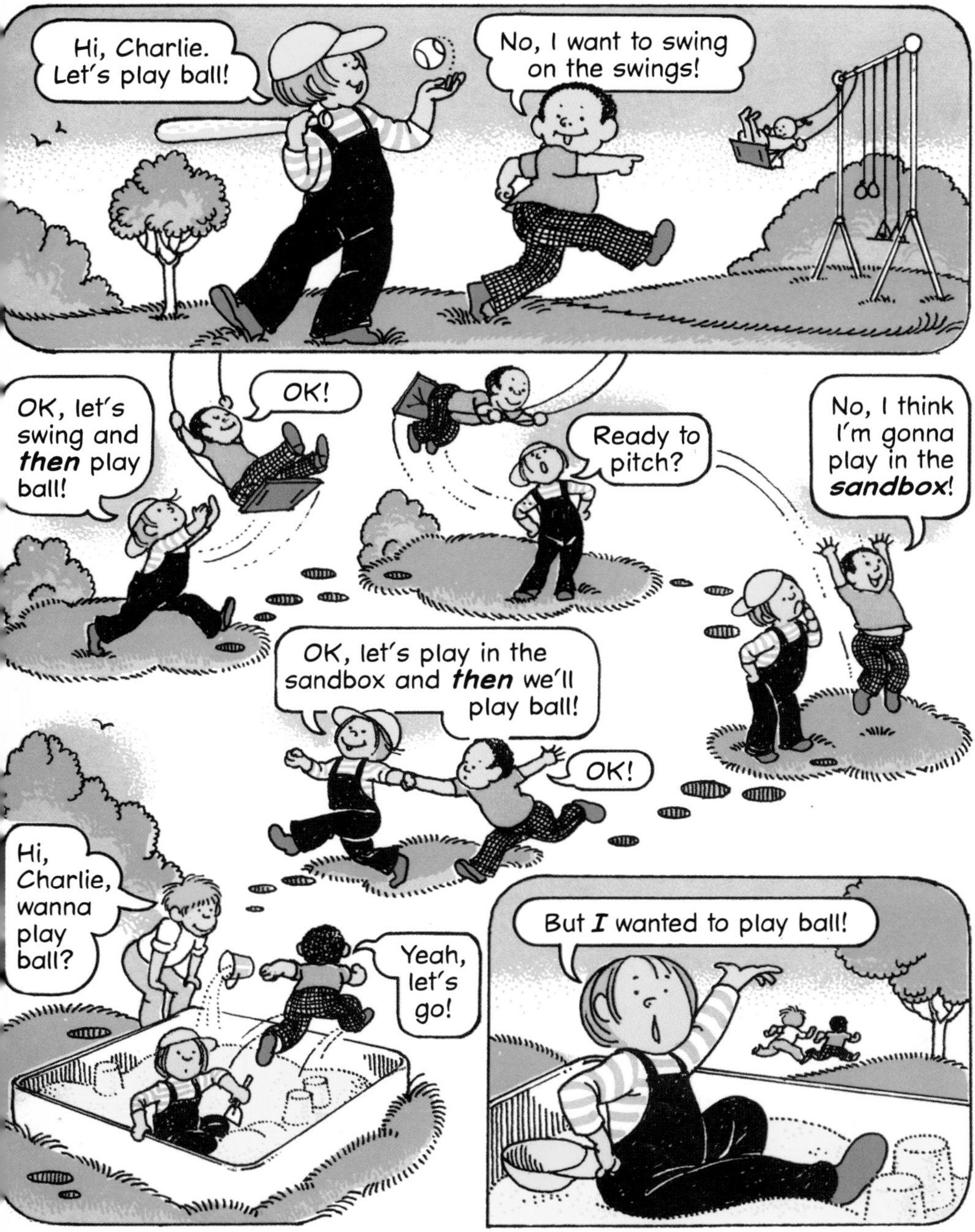
Hi, Charlie. Let's play ball!
No, I want to swing on the swings!
OK, let's swing and *then* play ball!
OK!
Ready to pitch?
No, I think I'm gonna play in the ***sandbox***!
OK, let's play in the sandbox and *then* we'll play ball!
OK!
Hi, Charlie, wanna play ball?
Yeah, let's go!
But *I* wanted to play ball!

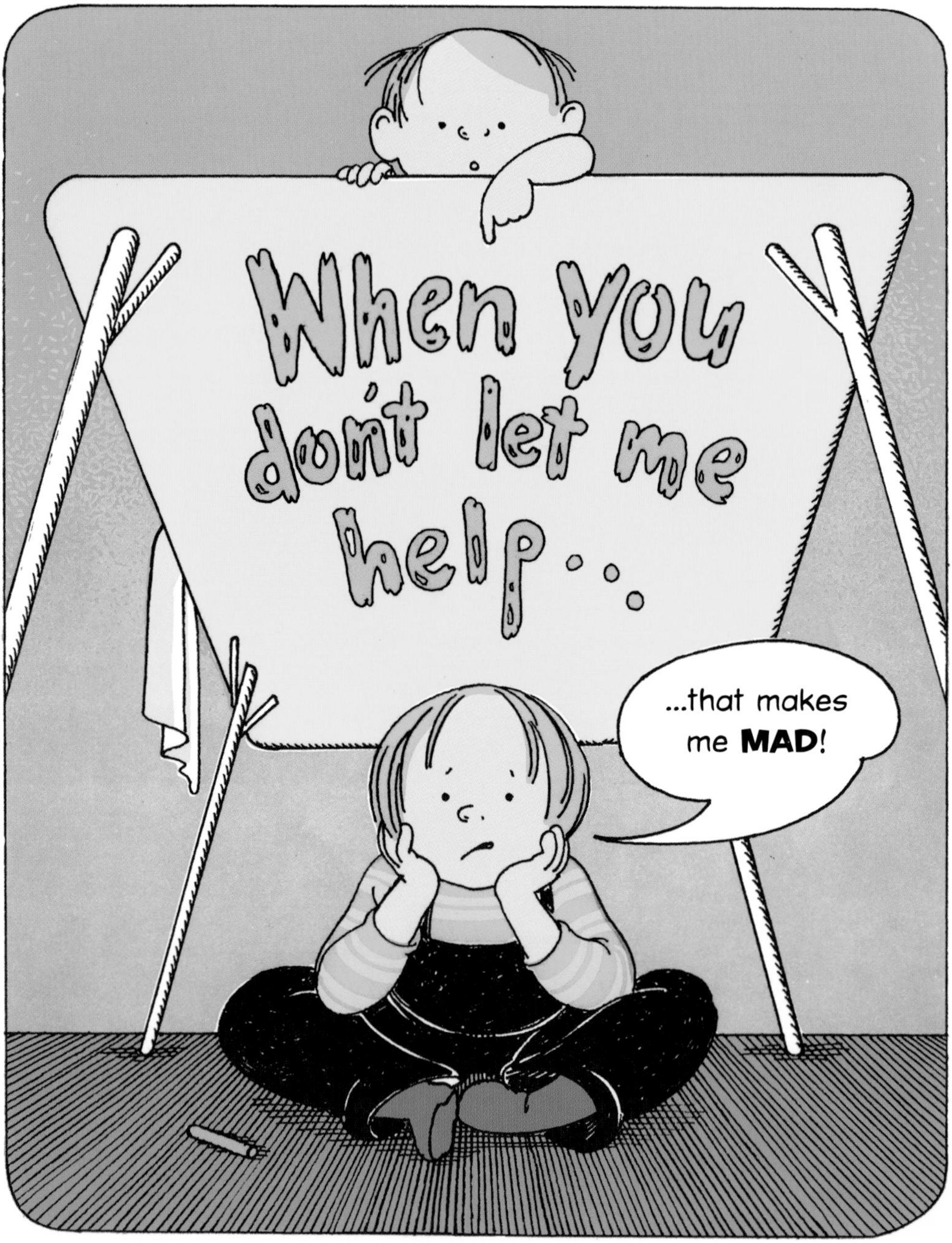
When you don't let me help...
...that makes me **MAD**!

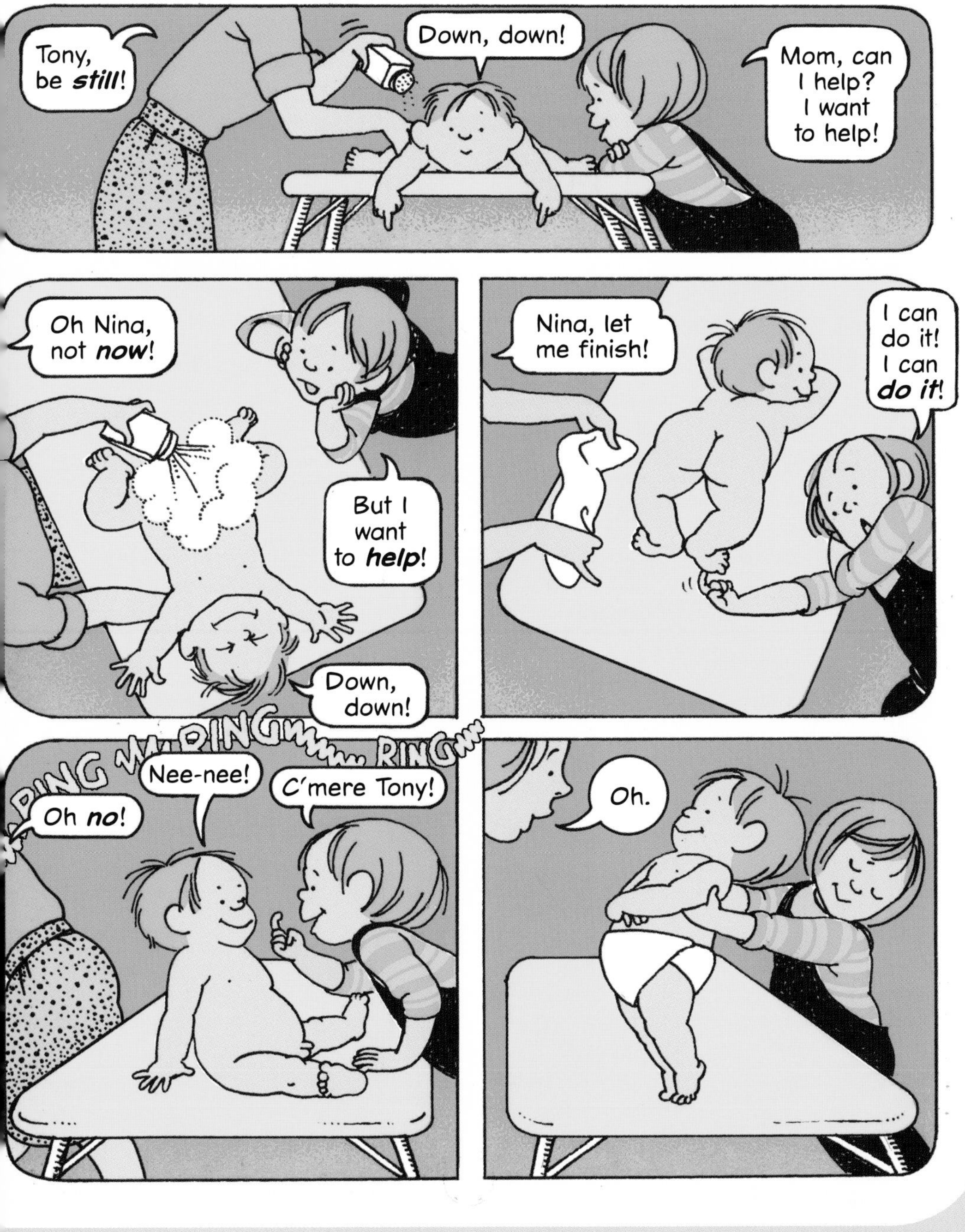
Tony, be *still*!
Down, down!
Mom, can I help? I want to help!
Oh Nina, not *now*!
But I want to *help*!
Down, down!
Nina, let me finish!
I can do it! I can *do it*!
RING RING RING
Oh *no*!
Nee-nee!
C'mere Tony!
Oh.

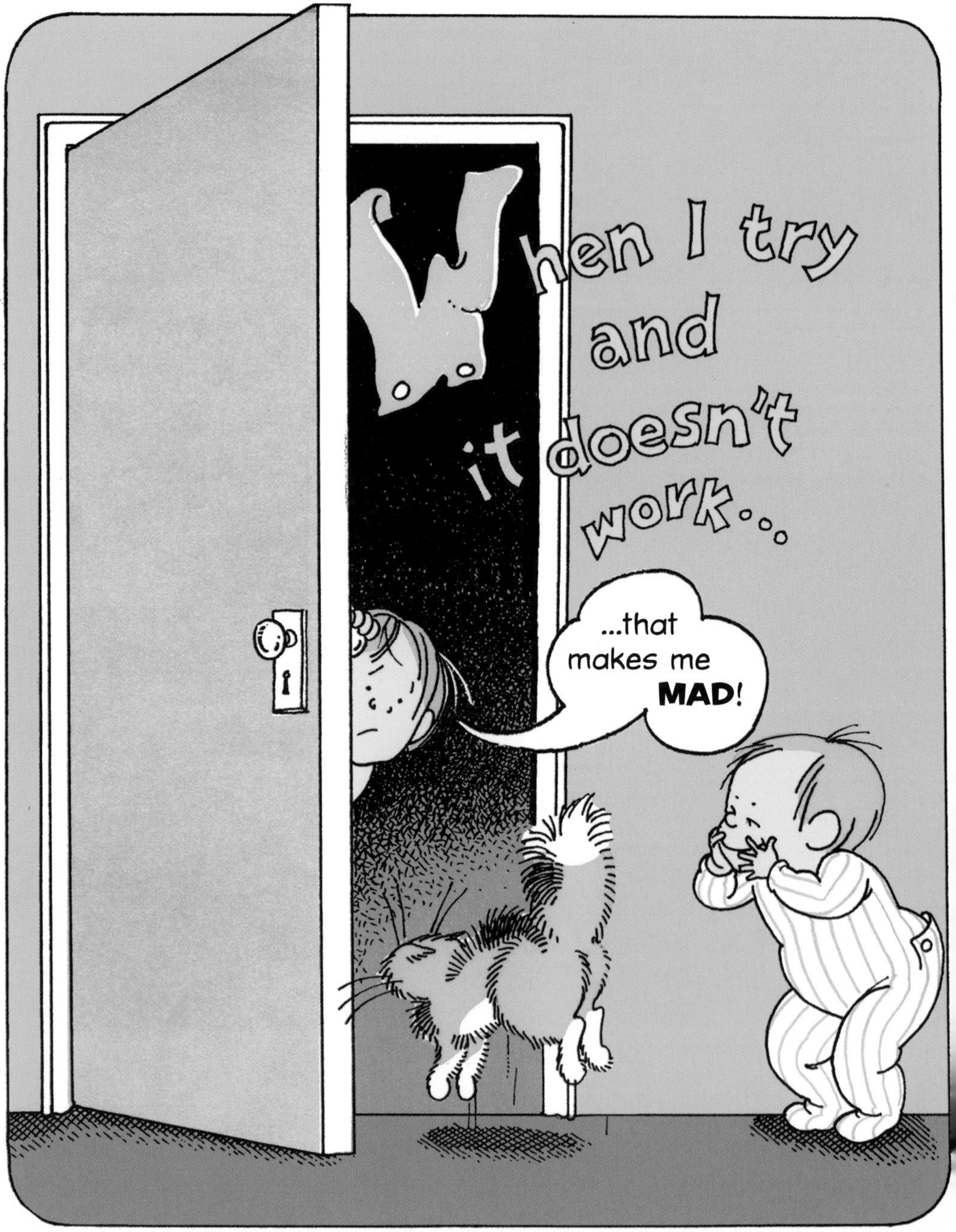
When I try and it doesn't work...
...that makes me MAD!

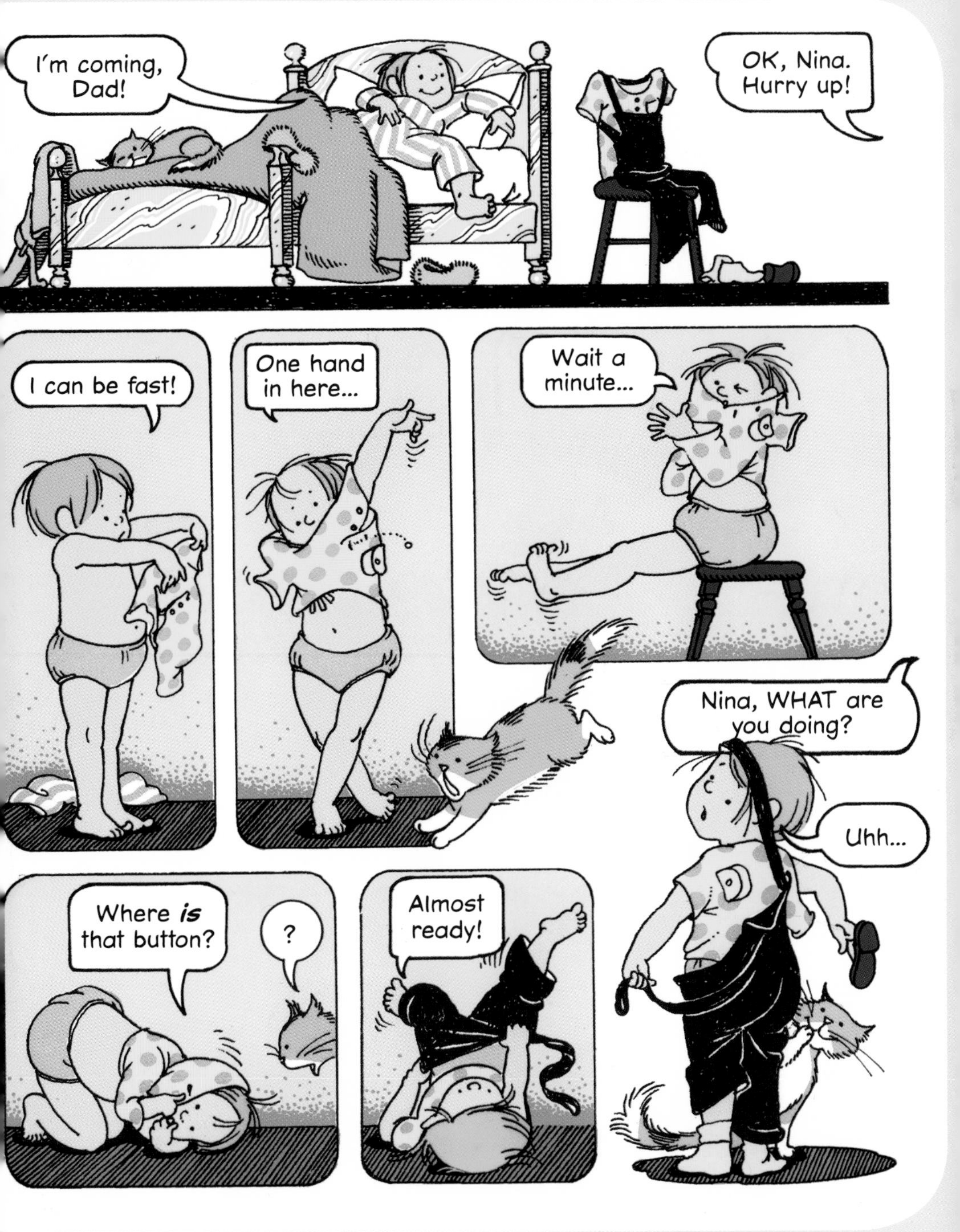
I'm coming, Dad!
OK, Nina. Hurry up!
I can be fast!
One hand in here...
Wait a minute...
Nina, WHAT are you doing?
Uhh...
Where *is* that button?
?
Almost ready!

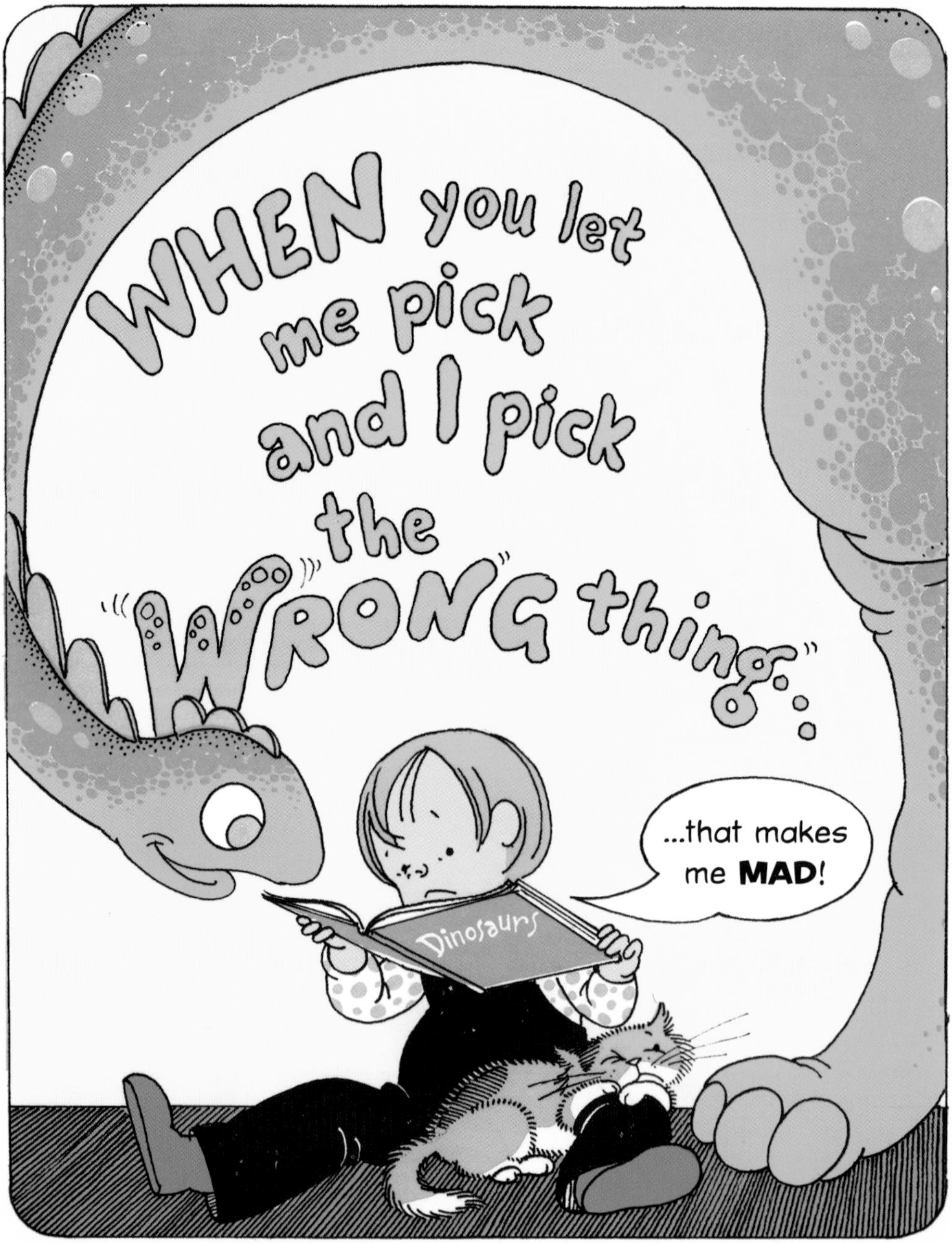
WHEN you let me pick and I pick the "WRONG thing"...
...that makes me **MAD**!
Dinosaurs

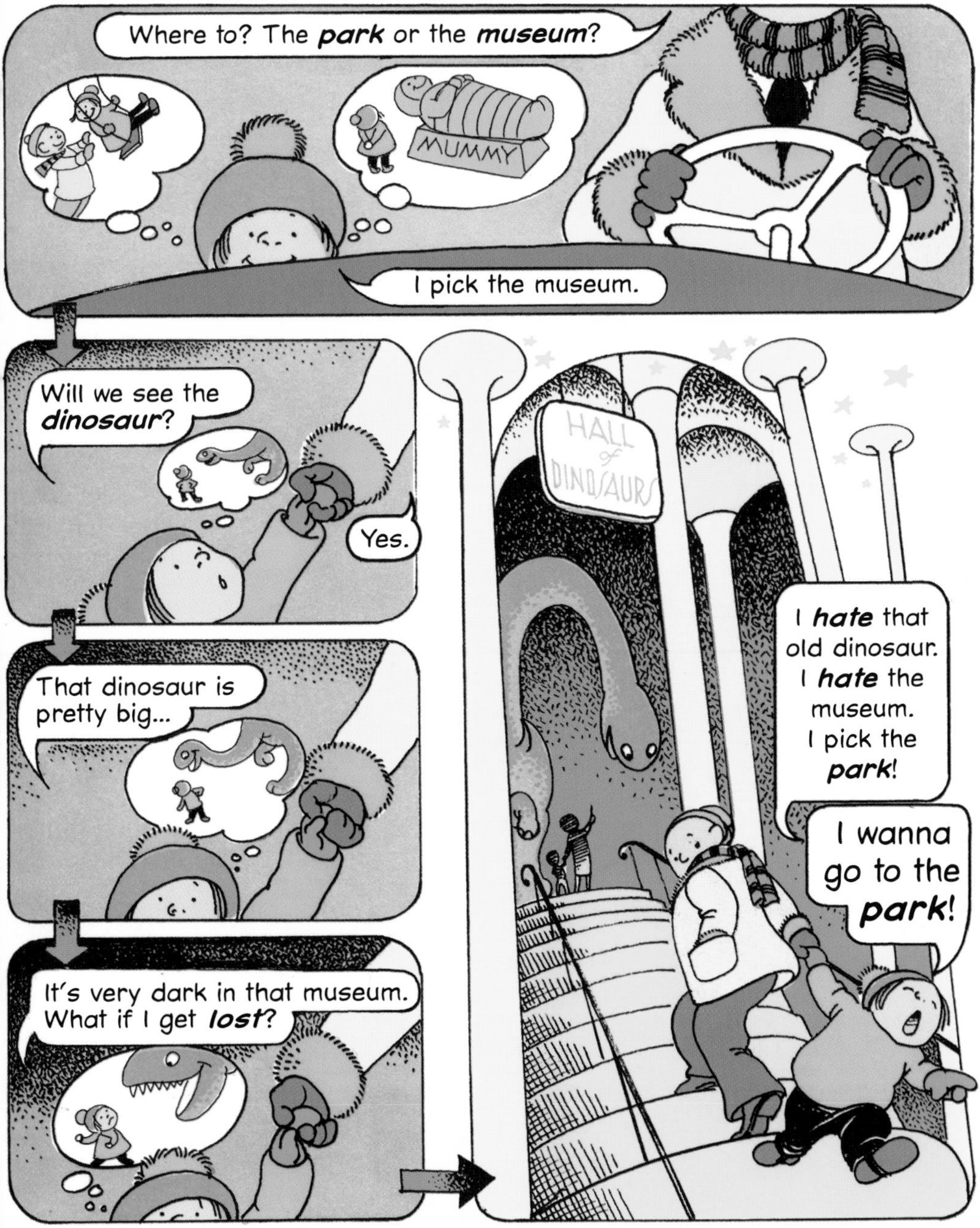
Where to? The **park** or the **museum**?
MUMMY
I pick the museum.
Will we see the **dinosaur**?
Yes.
That dinosaur is pretty big...
It's very dark in that museum. What if I get **lost**?
HALL of DINOSAURS
I **hate** that old dinosaur. I **hate** the museum. I pick the **park**!
I wanna go to the **park**!

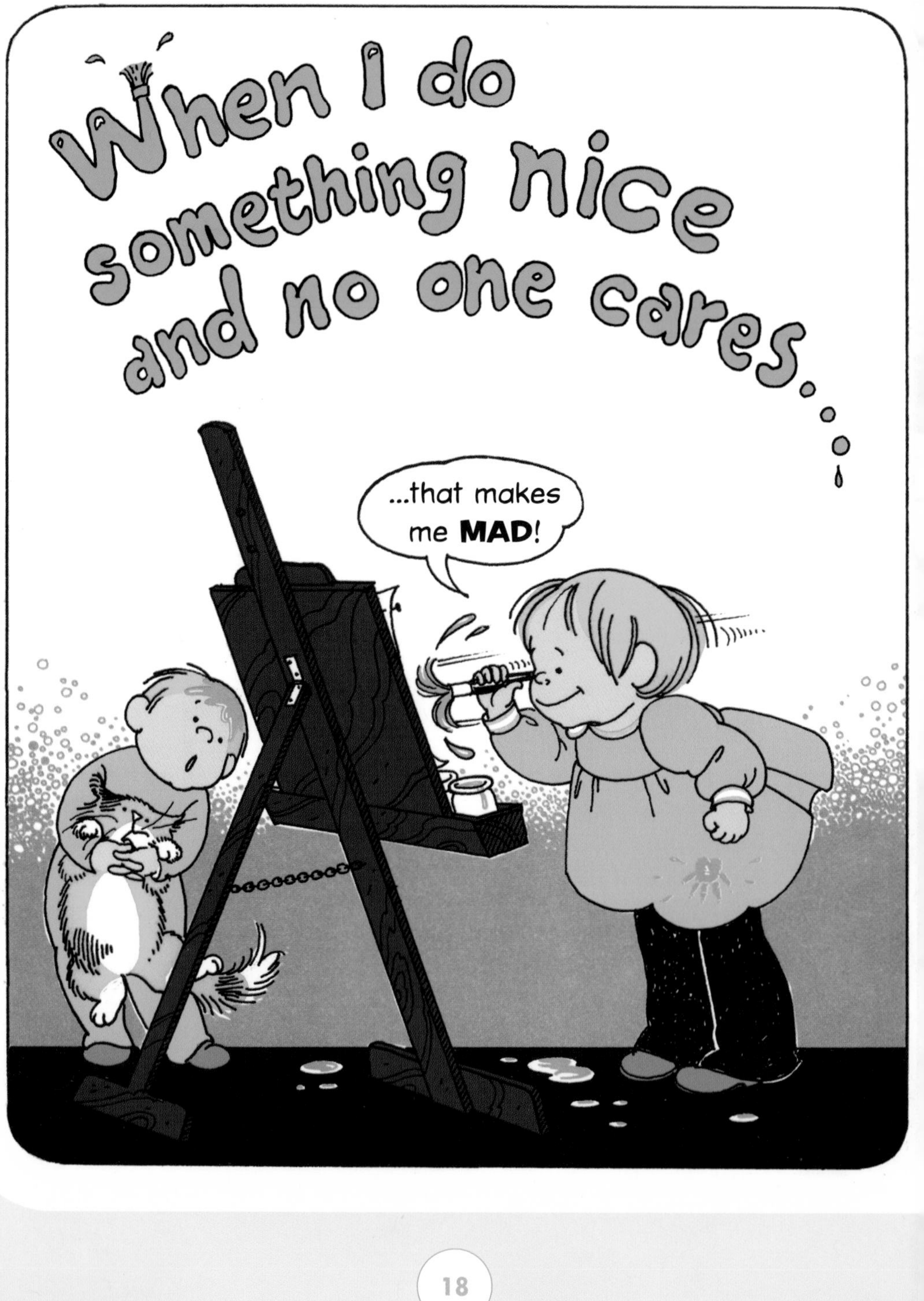
When I do something nice and no one cares...
...that makes me MAD!

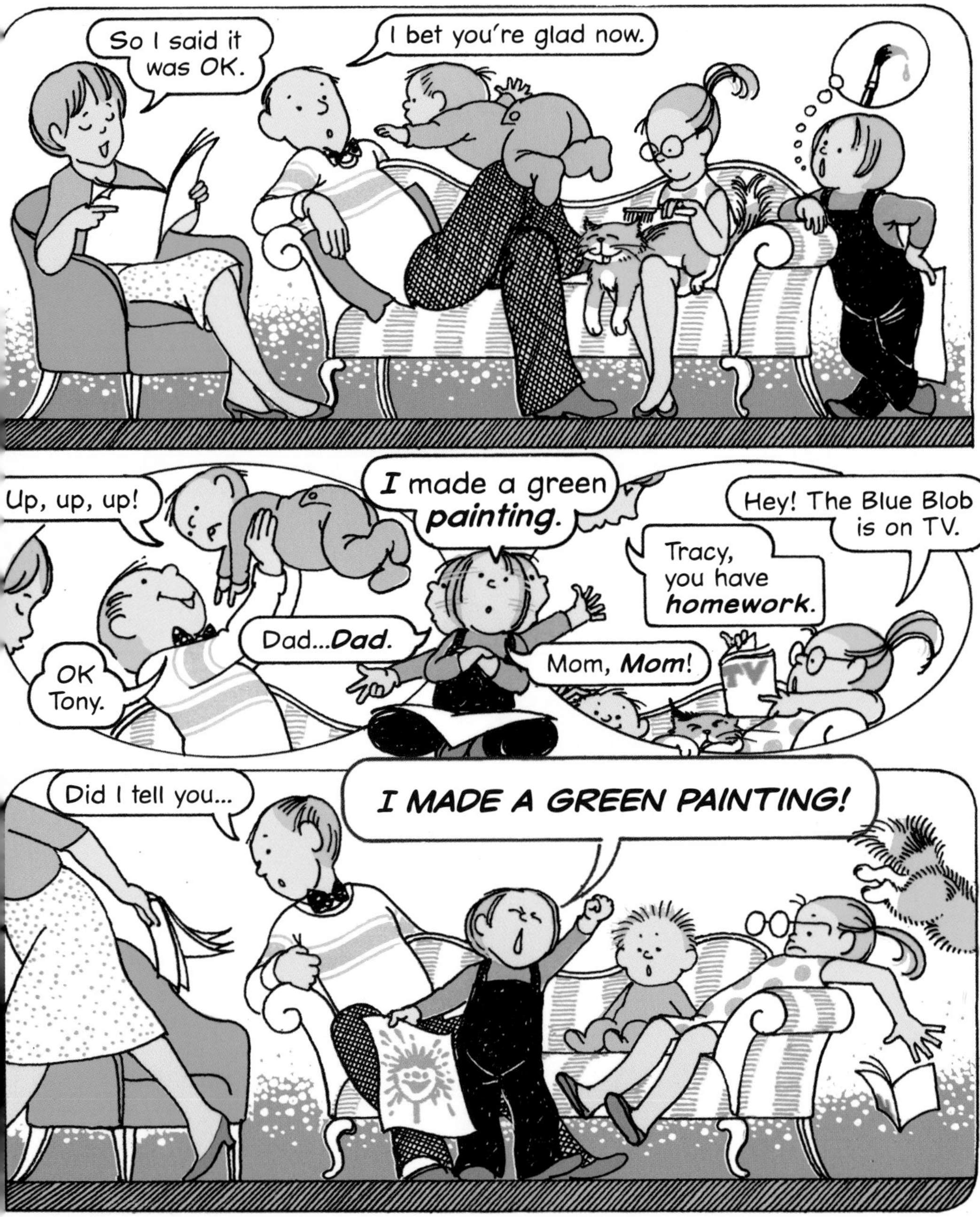
So I said it was OK.
I bet you're glad now.
Up, up, up!
I made a green painting.
Hey! The Blue Blob is on TV.
Tracy, you have homework.
OK Tony.
Dad...Dad.
Mom, Mom!
TV
Did I tell you...
I MADE A GREEN PAINTING!

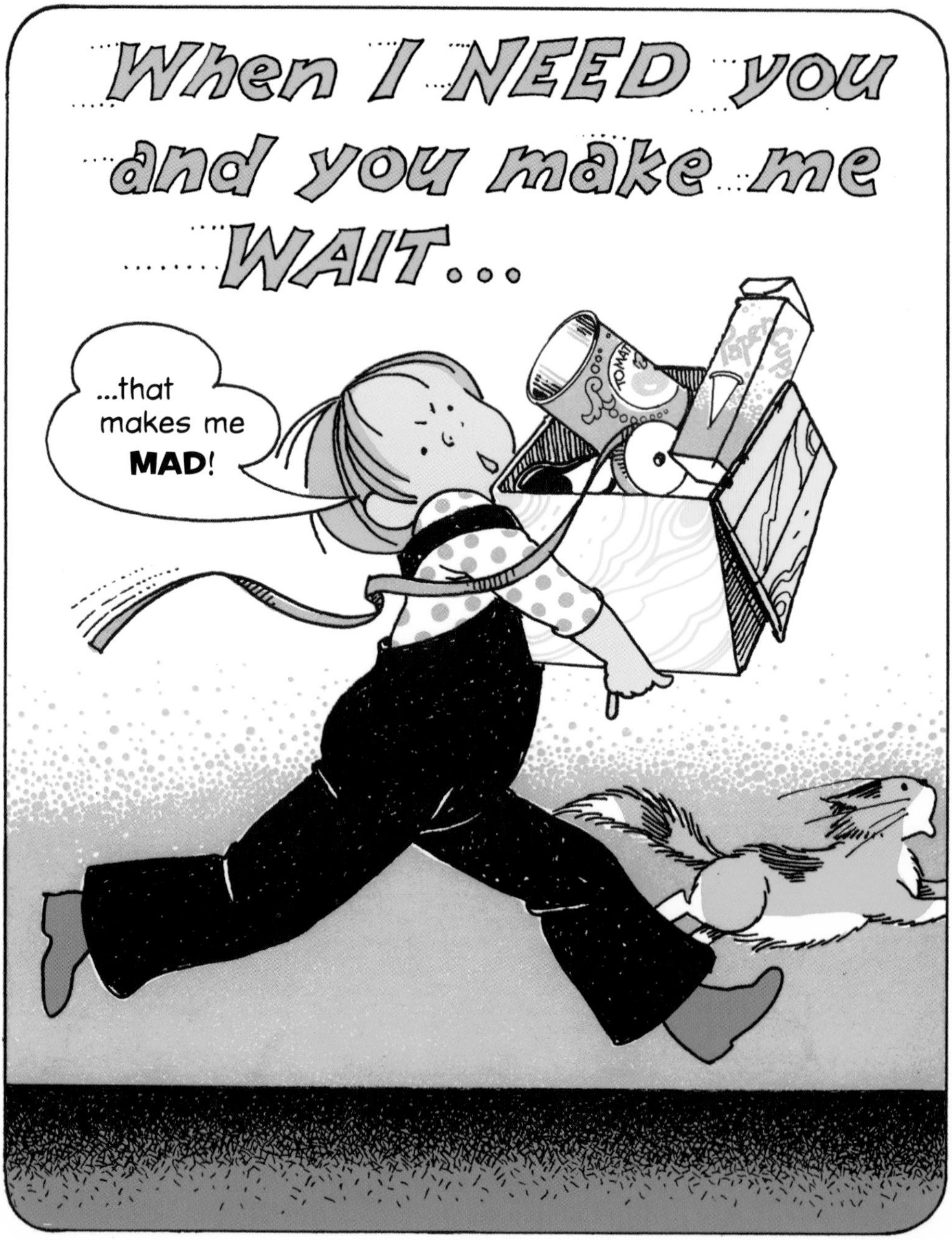
When I NEED you and you make me WAIT...
...that makes me **MAD**!
TOMATO
Paper Cup

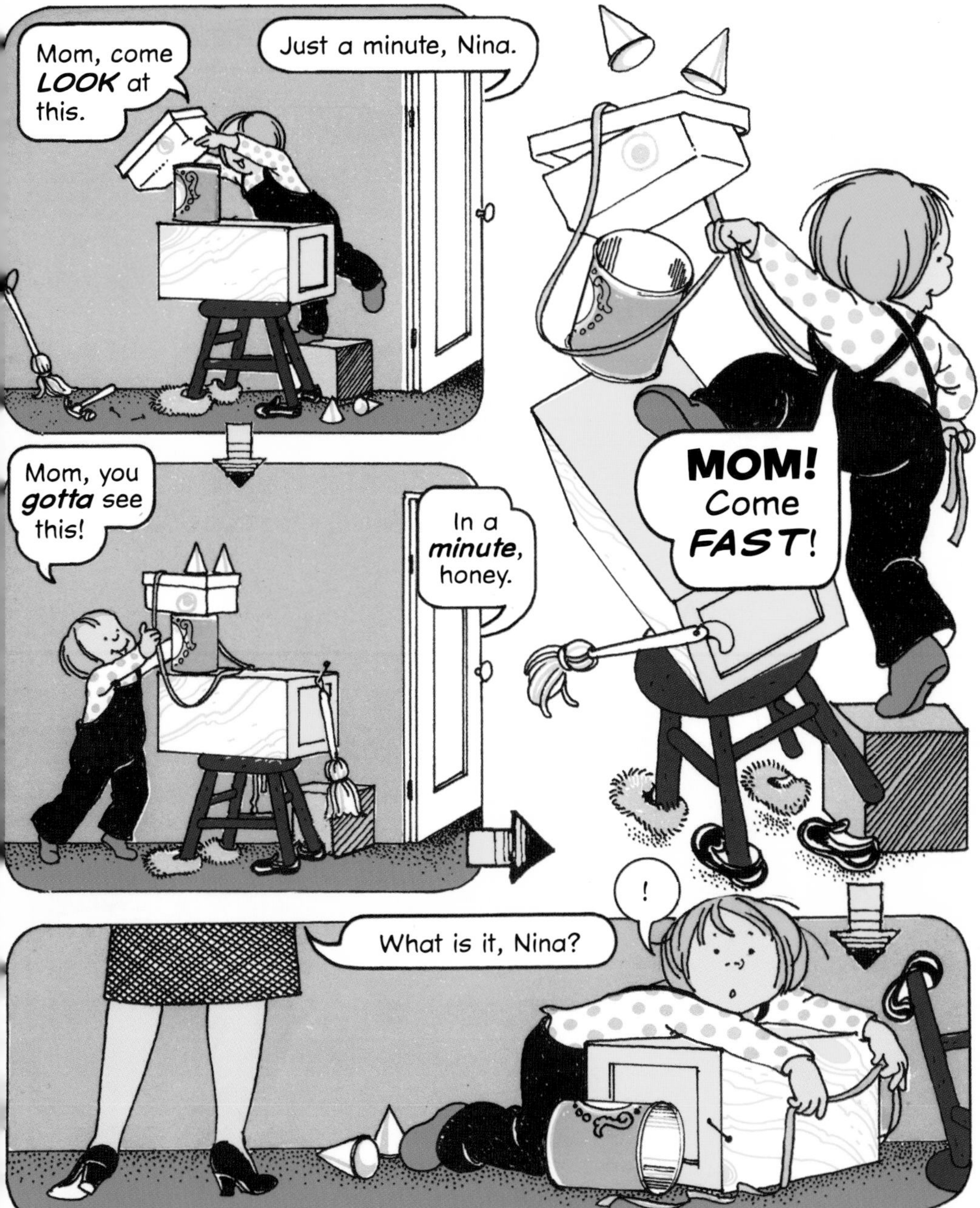

Mom, come **LOOK** at this.
Just a minute, Nina.
Mom, you *gotta* see this!
In a *minute*, honey.
MOM! Come ***FAST***!
What is it, Nina?
!

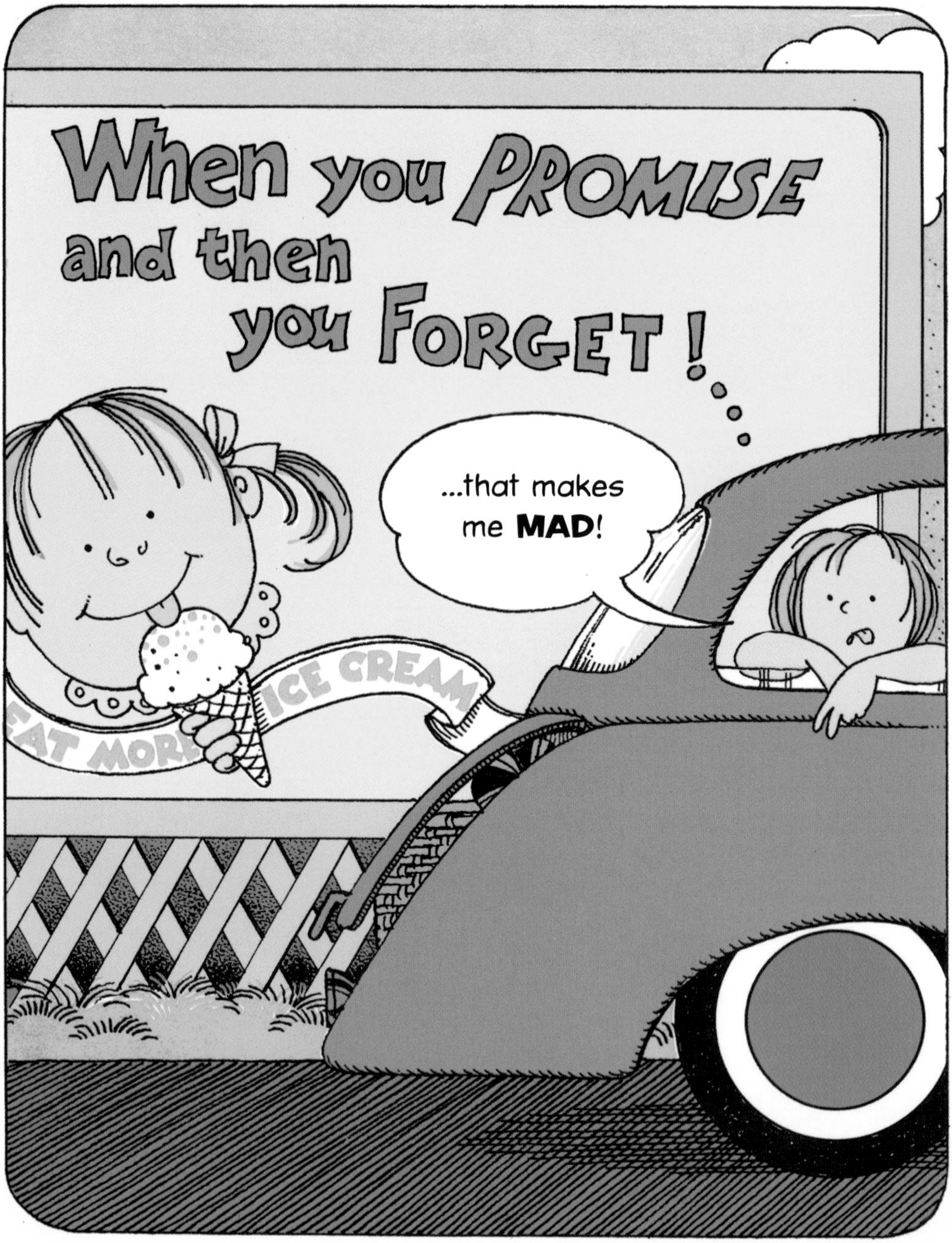
When you PROMISE and then you FORGET!...
...that makes me MAD!
EAT MORE ICE CREAM

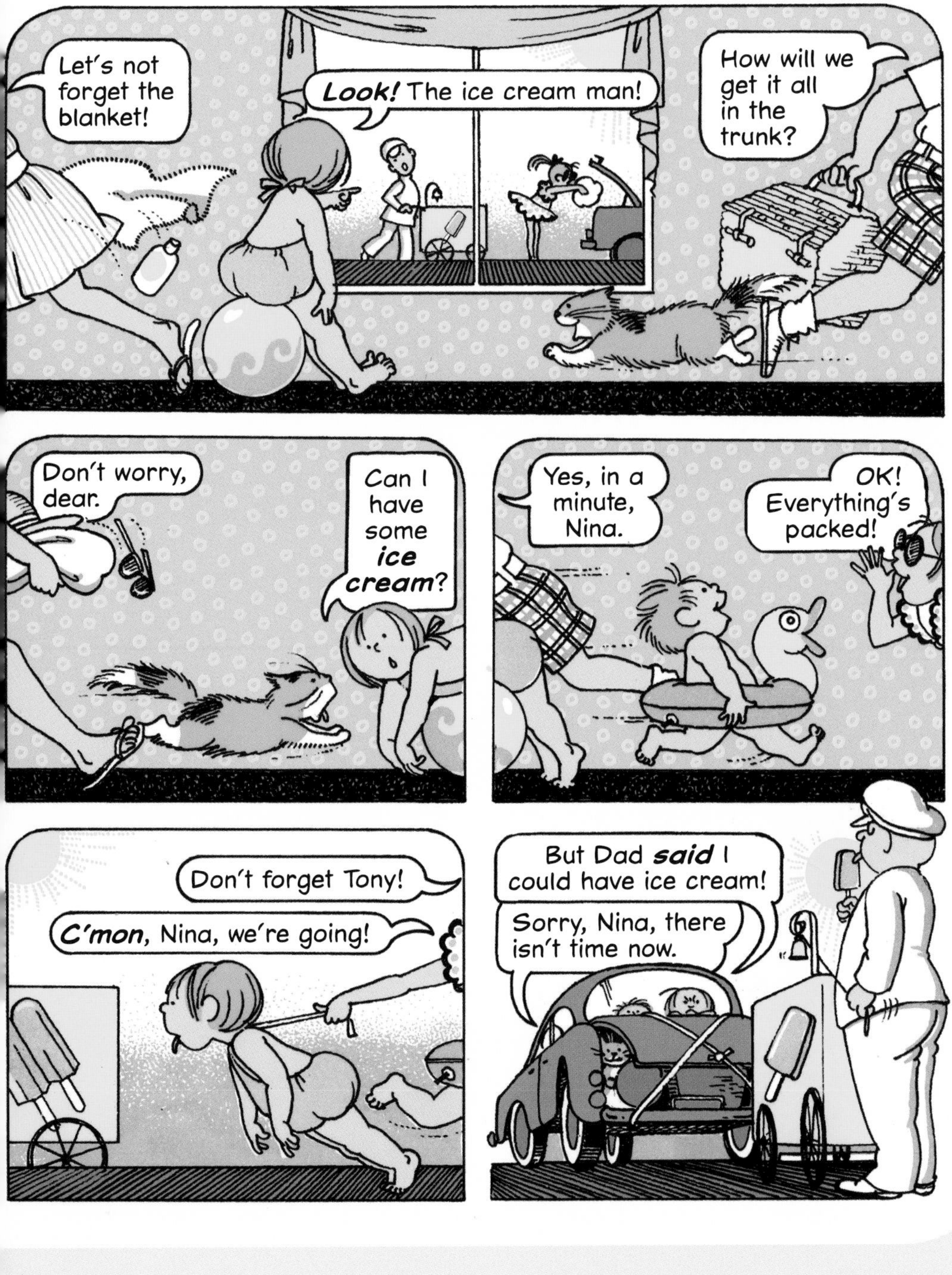
Let's not forget the blanket!
Look! The ice cream man!
How will we get it all in the trunk?
Don't worry, dear.
Can I have some *ice cream*?
Yes, in a minute, Nina.
OK! Everything's packed!
Don't forget Tony!
C'mon, Nina, we're going!
But Dad *said* I could have ice cream!
Sorry, Nina, there isn't time now.

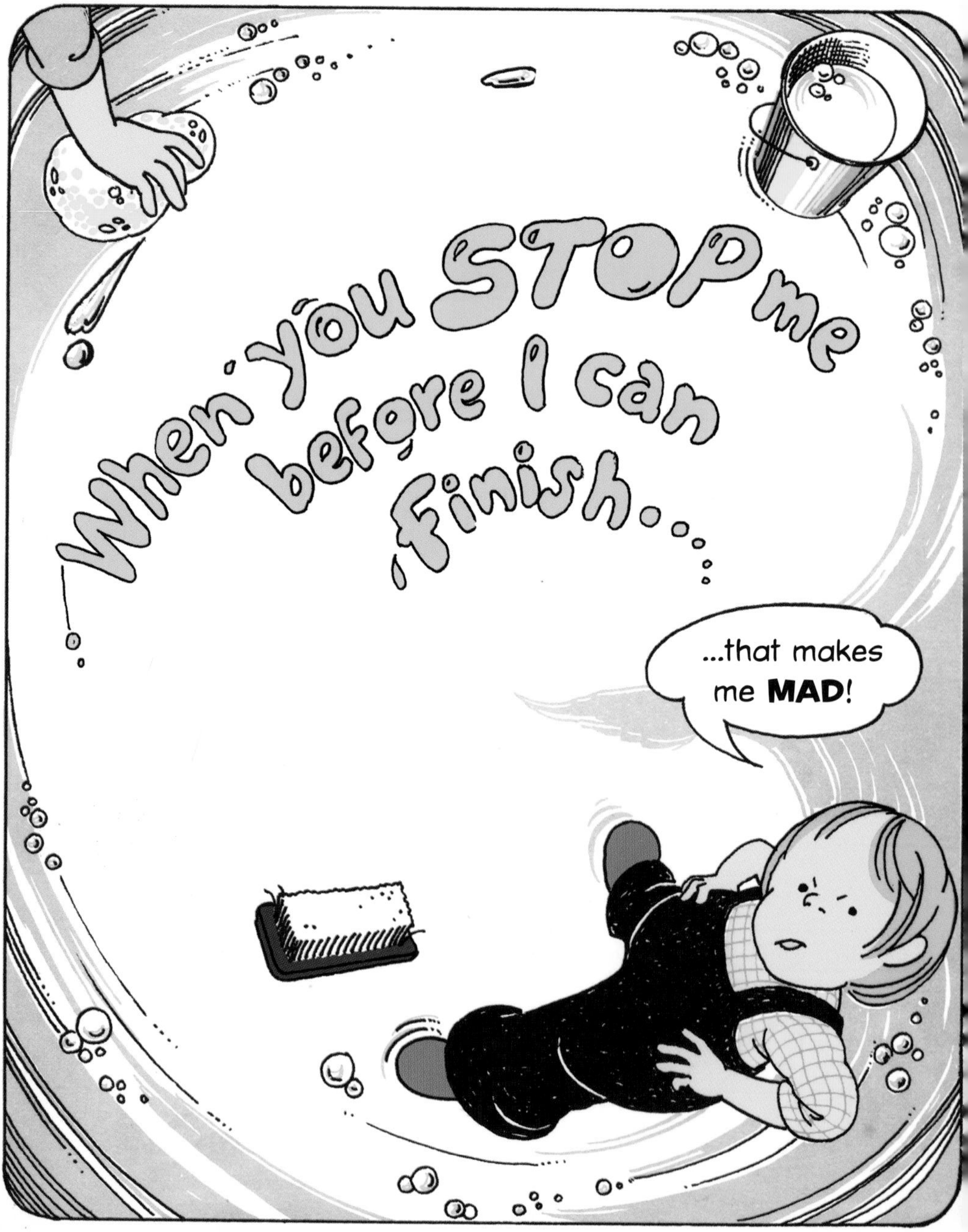
When you STOP me before I can finish...
...that makes me MAD!

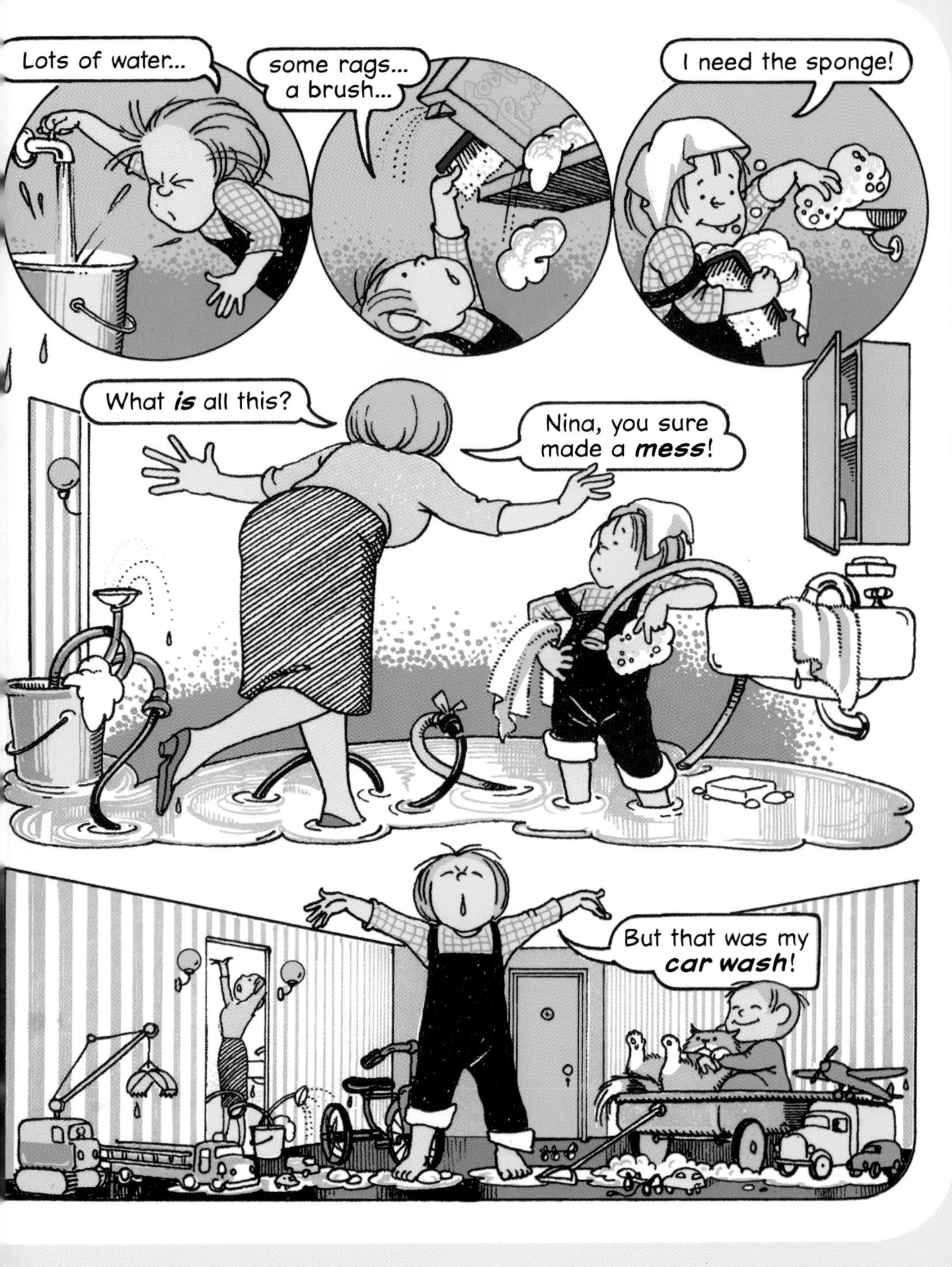
Lots of water...
some rags... a brush...
I need the sponge!
What *is* all this?
Nina, you sure made a **mess**!
But that was my **car wash**!

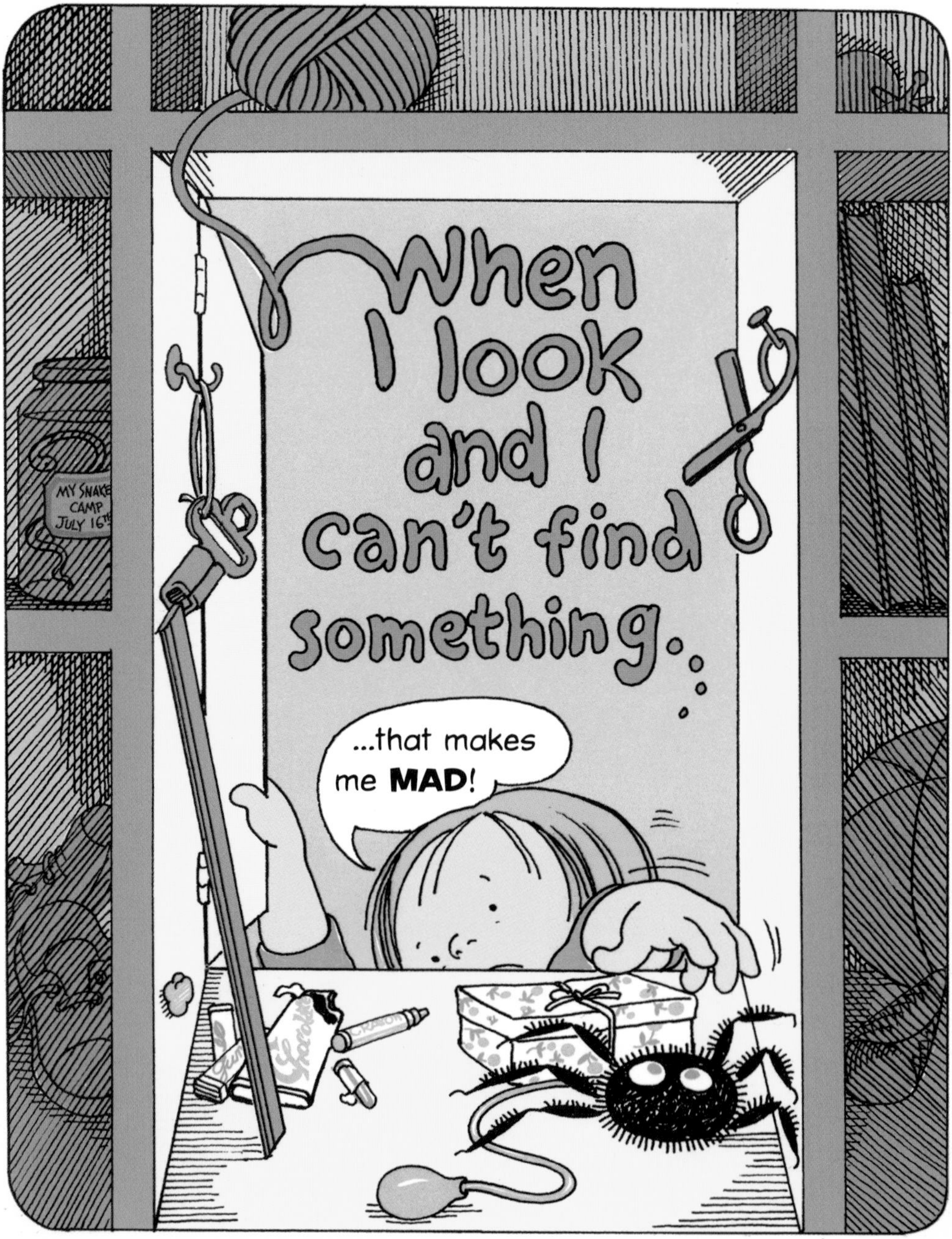
When I look and I can't find something...
...that makes me **MAD**!
MY SNAKE CAMP JULY 16TH

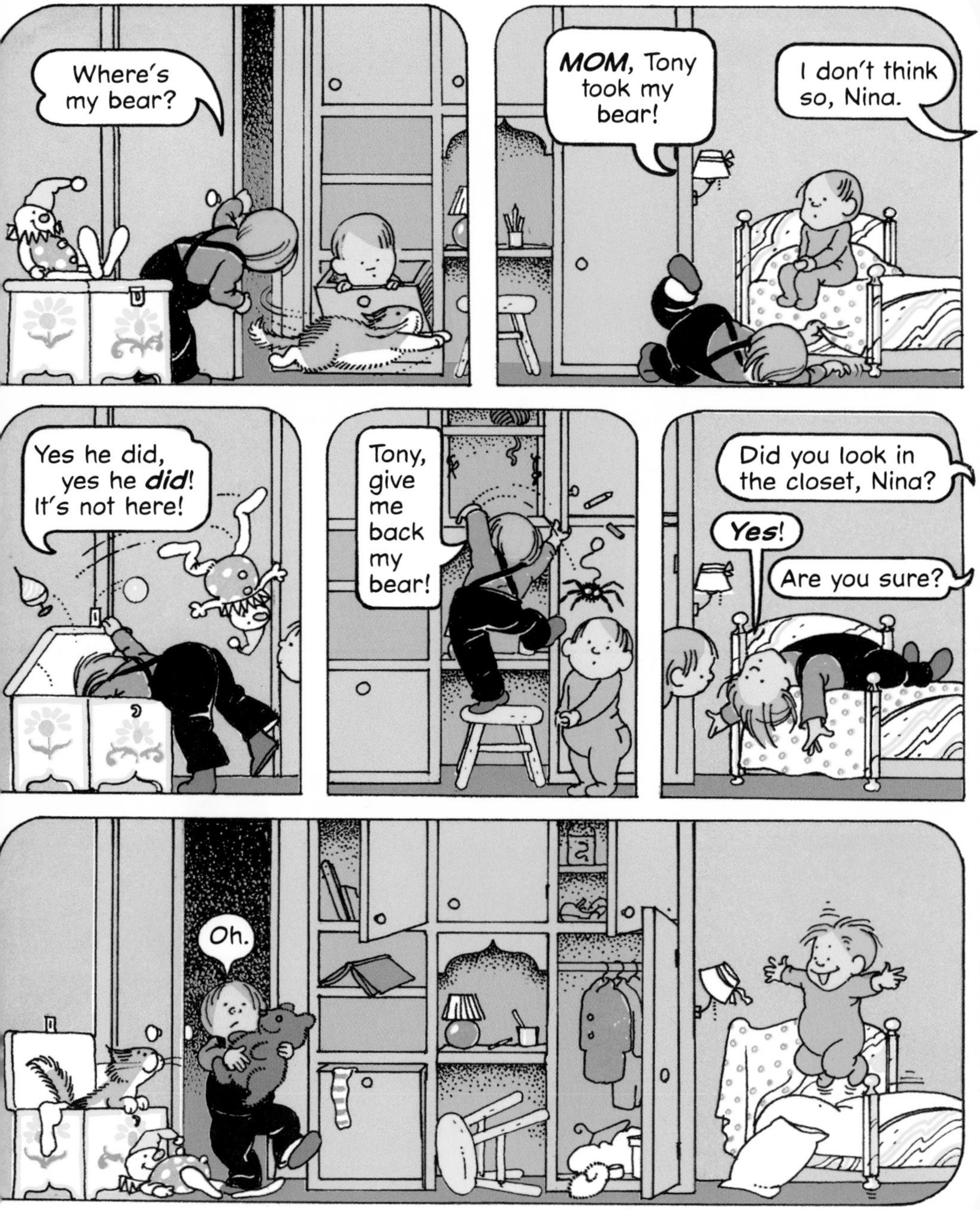
Where's my bear?
MOM, Tony took my bear!
I don't think so, Nina.
Yes he did, yes he did! It's not here!
Tony, give me back my bear!
Did you look in the closet, Nina?
Yes!
Are you sure?
Oh.

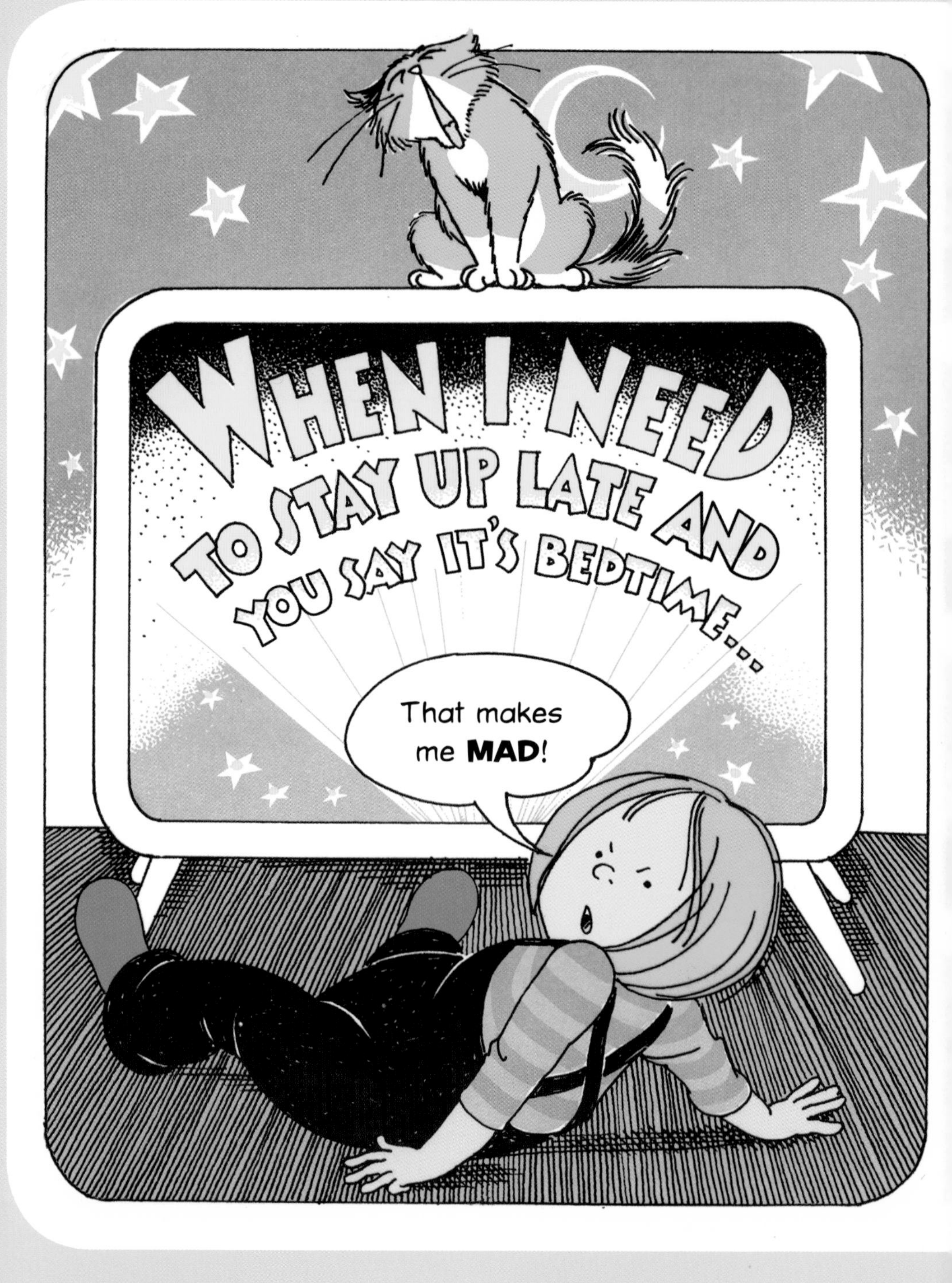
WHEN I NEED TO STAY UP LATE AND YOU SAY IT'S BEDTIME...
That makes me **MAD**!

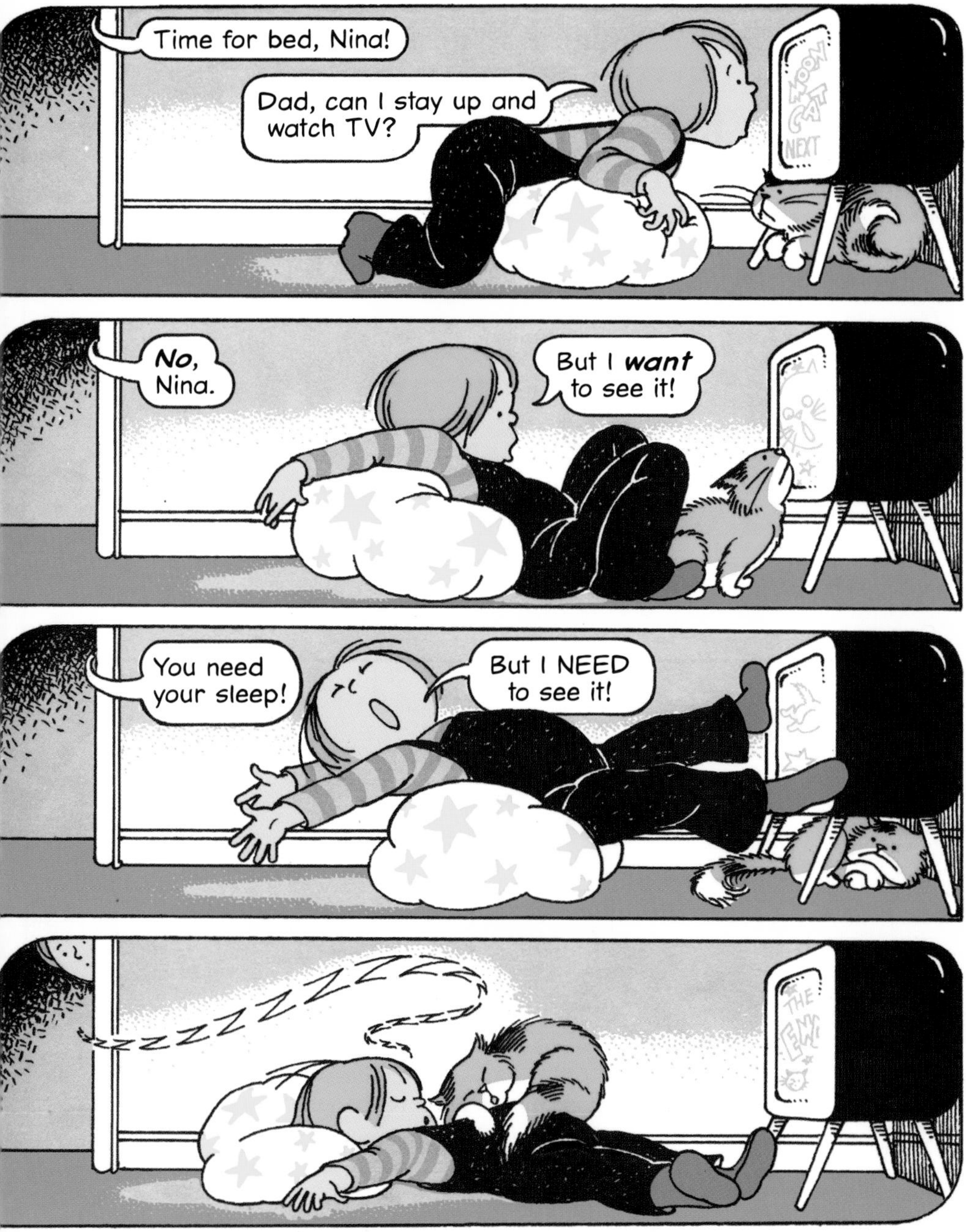
Time for bed, Nina!
Dad, can I stay up and watch TV?
MOON CAT NEXT
No, Nina.
But I want to see it!
You need your sleep!
But I NEED to see it!
THE

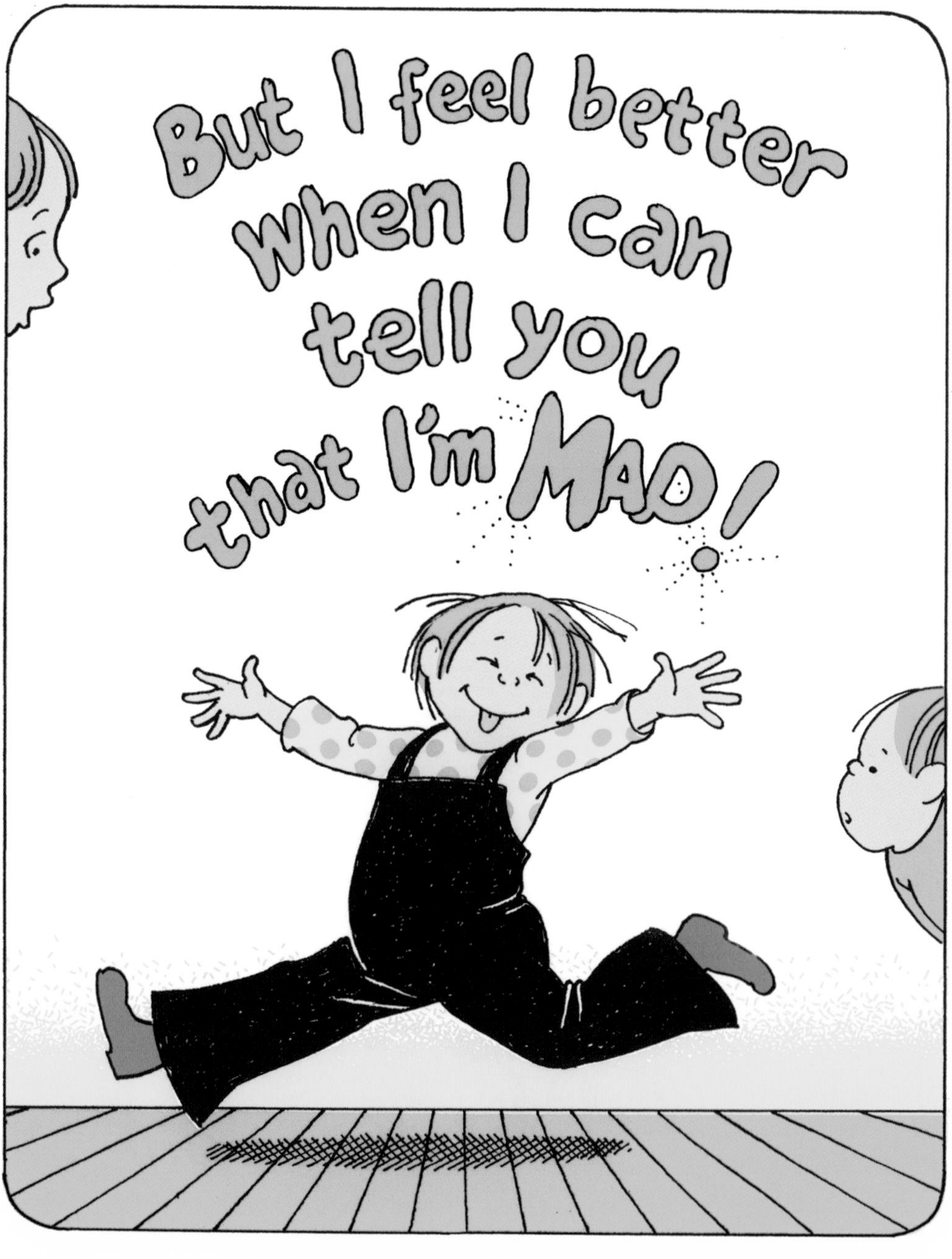
But I feel better
when I can
tell you
that I'm MAD!

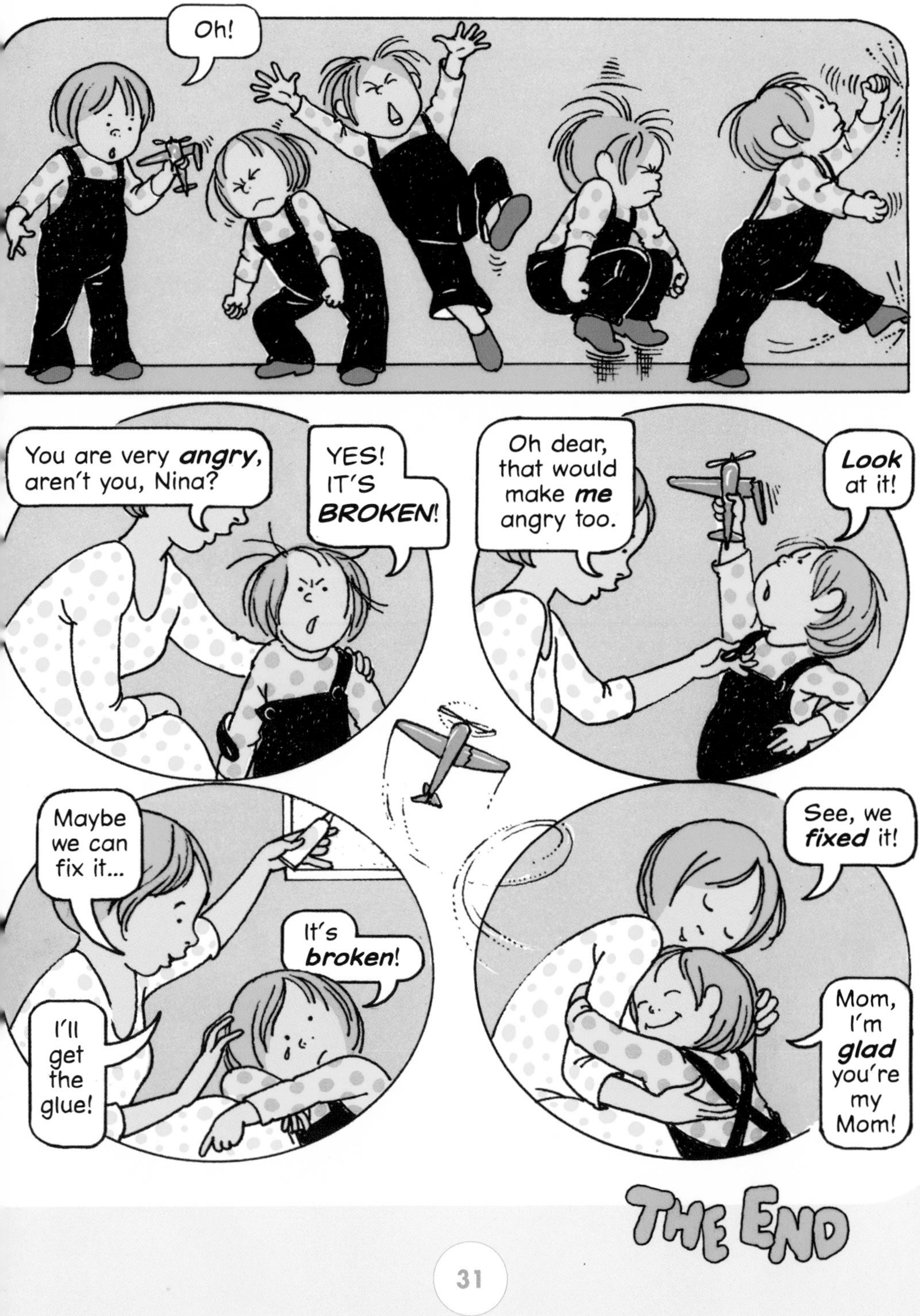
Oh!
You are very **angry**, aren't you, Nina?
YES! IT'S **BROKEN**!
Oh dear, that would make **me** angry too.
Look at it!
Maybe we can fix it...
It's **broken**!
I'll get the glue!
See, we **fixed** it!
Mom, I'm **glad** you're my Mom!
THE END

ABOUT THE AUTHORS

HILARY KNIGHT is the son of two accomplished artist-writers, Clayton Knight and Katherine Sturges, who collaborated on this classic *New Yorker* cover (Katherine penciled and Clayton inked it.) Hilary Knight came into his own enormous success by illustrating Kay Thompson's *Eloise,* which has been a cultural touchstone for generations. He has written and illustrated nine children's books and illustrated over fifty more. He has also produced many magazine illustrations, record-album covers, and posters for Broadway musicals.

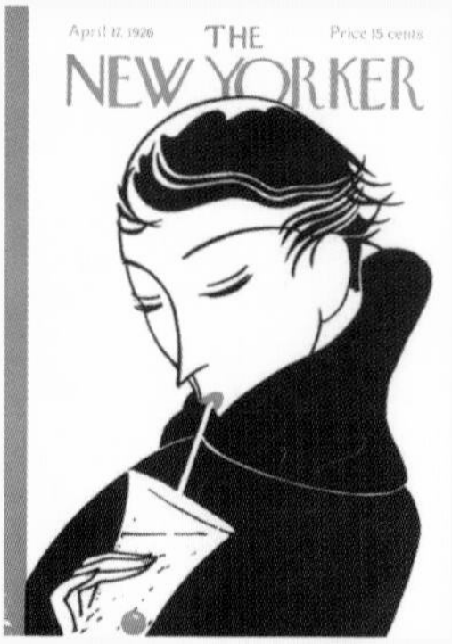
April 17, 1926
THE
Price 15 cents
NEW YORKER

STEVEN KROLL wrote nearly a hundred books for children. He has said, "When I'm working on a book, I see the pictures as I write the words. How fortunate that the illustrators of my books have all seen what I've seen and have captured the magic I wish to share."

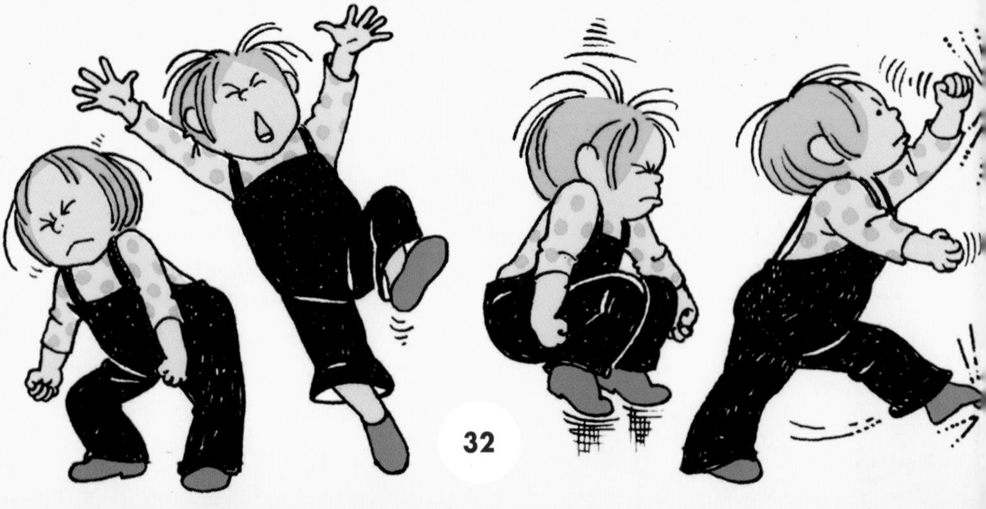

TIPS FOR PARENTS AND TEACHERS:

HOW TO READ COMICS WITH KIDS

Kids *love* comics! They are naturally drawn to the details in the pictures, which make them want to read the words. Comics beg for repeated readings and let both emerging and reluctant readers enjoy complex stories with a rich vocabulary. But since comics have their own grammar, here are a few tips for reading them with kids:

GUIDE YOUNG READERS: Use your finger to show your place in the text, but keep it at the bottom of the speaking character so it doesn't hide the very important facial expressions.

HAM IT UP! Think of the comic book story as a play and don't hesitate to read with expression and intonation. Assign parts or get kids to supply the sound effects, a great way to reinforce phonics skills.

LET THEM GUESS. Comics provide a lot of context for the words, so the emerging readers can make informed guesses. Like jigsaw puzzles, comics ask readers to make connections, so check a young audience's understanding by asking "What's this character thinking?" (but don't be surprised if a kid finds some of the comics' subtle details faster than you).

TALK ABOUT THE PICTURES. Point out how the artist paces the story with pauses (silent panels) or speeded-up action (a burst of short panels). Discuss how the size and shape of the panels carry meaning.

ABOVE ALL, ENJOY! There is of course never one right way to read, so go for the shared pleasure. Once children make the story happen in their imagination, they have discovered the thrill of reading, and you won't be able to stop them. At that point, just go get them more books, and more comics.

www.TOON-BOOKS.com

SEE OUR FREE ONLINE CARTOON MAKERS,
LESSON PLANS, AND MUCH MORE

TOON INTO READING

LEVEL 1

GRADES K–1

LEXILE BR–100 • GUIDED READING E–G • READING RECOVERY 7–10

FIRST COMICS FOR BRAND-NEW READERS

- 200–300 easy sight words
- short sentences
- often one character
- single time frame or theme
- 1–2 panels per page

LEVEL 2

GRADES 1–2

LEXILE BR–170 • GUIDED READING G–J • READING RECOVERY 11–17

EASY-TO-READ COMICS FOR EMERGING READERS

- 300–600 words
- short sentences and repetition
- story arc with few characters in a small world
- 1–4 panels per page

LEVEL 3

GRADES 2–3

LEXILE 150–300 • GUIDED READING J–N • READING RECOVERY 17–19

CHAPTER-BOOK COMICS FOR ADVANCED BEGINNERS

- 800–1000+ words in long sentences
- broad world as well as shifts in time and place
- long story divided in chapters
- reader needs to make connections and speculate